PHOENIX

PHOENIX

A novel by Melissa Pritchard

CANE HILL PRESS

Library of Congress Number: 91-71514

ISBN No. 0-943433-08-8

Cover art by Louise Hamlin

Published by Cane Hill Press
225 Varick Street
New York, N.Y. 10014

Produced at The Print Center., Inc., 225 Varick St.,
New York, NY 10014, a non-profit facility for literary
and arts-related publications. (212) 206-8465

For my daughters
Noelle Victoria
and
Caitlin Skye

"*Now I am going in for debauch. Why? I want to be a poet, and I am working to make myself a Visionary: you won't possibly understand, and I don't know how to explain it to you. To arrive at the unknown through the disordering of all the senses, that's the point. The suffering will be tremendous, but one must be strong, be born a poet: it is in no way my fault.*"

Rimbaud

PHOENIX

You park your hair behind your ears, plug it in a ponytail, wear old pants, an ugly coat, act all chuggy with cuss and spit, they'll leave you alone.

Hitching doesn't scare me. If you go about it right—it's moving through stories, riding with people, each one a chapter, a color.

"I invented the color of vowels! —A Black, E White, I Red, O Blue, U Green ... at first, it was an experiment. I wrote silences, I wrote the night. I recorded the inexpressible."

Rimbaud

I am covered in deliberate plainness. Also silence.

Journeybook
October
1969

Swaying from the silver-blue rearview mirror, knees tucked, hands lifting jet hair, breasts no-nippled, no jiggling like real life, ticking brainless with the truck, a hula doll in a green skirt like lawn clippings strung together …

Phoenix, elusive under semi-parted flaps of frizzly hair, in a crumpled work shirt, cut-offs, hiking boots without laces or socks, is tranced by the road-sway of the hula doll, so plugged into this truck she almost forgets to bail out at the Lompoc exit. She'd hiked into his cab stoned; hard to roust herself, get down, start over.

Thanks guy, she addresses Mr. Potato in sunglasses. Much obliged. Splays her fingers in a V.

Yeah, peace yourself. Peace, Love, Filth. I bet there's a pretty young lady under that hippie trash. Too bad you're not cleaned up. I'd take you to dinner, go dancing, have us a good time.

Phoenix drags her pack off the seat, nods toward the doll. You might want to take her out sometime.

He's half on the highway by the time she whomps the door. The truck wheels blow gravel as he aims for Lompoc with a load of whatever. She hadn't asked.

She's hardly out when a lichen green VW bus clunks to an idle a ways up on the shoulder; she trots up to it.

The driver's a chopstick-skinny dude in a leather vest, with a squirrel-bush ponytail. The old lady's his twin except for dangly temple bell earrings. The van lets out a humongous belch of dope as she throws in her pack.

A grin trips over Squirrel-woman's face as she hands back the butt end of a joint to Phoenix who tokes absently before flipping it out the window, fingertips burning.

They buzz along flat ocean, gull feathers and amber beads swinging from the van's mirror. Meher Baba's picture is crookedly duct-taped to the dash, an avatar keeping forty years Silence. She's not impressed. Anybody can keep quiet, do the scam of eloquent Silence. She does it all the time. Baba has a pillowy face, licorice whip mustache. An Italian high-wire artist.

Deadpan, grinding ocean. People geographically naive to the sea romanticize its anxious aluminum glaze, a monotonous hurl and suck she's spent her entire life beside, riding in cars, mobile temples with dashboard shrines. Her first car, her one car, a pink '47 Cadillac, got heisted before she could tie one feather or bead to it. She'd bought a car to run away in, lent it out the first day to some guy from Venice Beach, never saw him or it again. Right now her mother was probably cruising the family car, looking for her. Maybe coming up behind them. Maybe not.

Santa Barbara. She's dropped at a beachside park, sits in rancid sunlight before a bandstand like a halved egg, yolk popped, the hollow madonna blue. On the stage, bums, winos, splayed like a hand of cards except one guy propped against the scooped wall, legs whistled out, another shuffling, fwapping his hands as if shaking off water or blood. The rest clasp hands, humble necks drooped. She's close enough to hear hollering, praying, confessing, singing would be nice—what she does make out is somebody hawking phlegm. She should step up there. Participate. Our Lady of Winos and Vagrants. Because of these men, meekly slouched, Phoenix digs out a green cloth journal from her pack, recording their cryptic sweet assembly before walking up State Street.

The city drops in a graceful ochre-roofed decline from golden foothills to this boulevard, a thin seaside crimping of motels, pancake houses, seafood restaurants, the air thick with fried foods, auto exhaust, ocean brine. Palm trees butt against pearly sidewalks, latticed elephant legs, bladed fronds clumped with orangeish balls, plastic fruit on a bonnet. Nearest the beach, Lower State is a coarse linkage of thrift shops, flop hotels, used car lots, botulus diners. Phoenix buys a sandwich at a Greek deli, sits on a Moorish tiled planter across from a Salvation Army mission house. Love Never Faileth in white, scabbing off the arched entrance. Her teeth squeak into the tough, oil-soaked bread as she observes sudden, heavy commotion nearby. A swarm of burlapped, white-faced freaks flows around her, except for one dwarfish creature sinking on his knees to tug a bite off her sand-

4

wich. His grease paint gicks up her crust. God, how does she do it? Attract the weirdest ones. Always, every time.

−na see a play? The words are stuffed with salami. When he leans in to poach a second bite, Phoenix whips the sandwich up over his somewhat oversized head.

Why?

We have a show to perform in ten minutes. Tragically, we possess no audience.

Why?

We do dangerous anti-war material, we are the fatal cure for a town of wealthy, freeze-dried Republicans. Like pure artists, we are not admired or applauded. Admission is free. Five minutes till curtain.

She lowers her arm, which he seizes, ripping off another bite of sandwich.

Rounded-up vagrants, winos, dismantled sorts, herself, file up stairs into a theater, strangely hidden in an abandoned office building. Matte black, tiny, it's like being inside a small simple camera. The audience fills in the rows of black wooden seats. The dim house lights go out entirely.

Red glare on a vacant stage. The same burlapped, white-faced creatures she had seen on the street roll in from the wings, atonally noisy, grotesquely posturing. Horrid moanings emerge from four beings, encased like blue pupa, and caroming across the stage floor, to vanish howling into the wings. In the downstage left corner, an actor, hair like bleached tumbleweed, in a woman's bathing suit with protruding sponge falsies, recites in falsetto from Bertrand Russell's letters. The audience responds with a crackling of paper around the tipped necks of bottles, with much vocal bewilderment. The end, prematurely applauded twice, receives slurry huzzahs, hollers. Her friend hops off the stage, comes up to her, cowl flipped back, a tiny, spooky apostle.

What'd you think?

I think I didn't get it.

That's because it's original. Inspired by Grotowski. It probably needs polish. Probably needs Grotowski. Tomorrow's our final performance, then we're kicked out of here. If you'll come tomorrow, I'll save you the same seat.

Thanks but I'm headed north.

Oh, loss.

Six dollars is fine, she says to the desk clerk, whose scalp shines like stretched bubble gum under maroon spriggings of hair. The clerk's face clamps and tightens on Phoenix, the stained work shirt, frizzly unwashed hair, leather headband.

I want no trouble, which spells NO GENTLEMEN in the room. I get aggravation from all the damn winos without you hippie types on top of it.

Phoenix palms the key off the counter. I ain't a hippie, ma' am, swear on a stack of Arkansas Bibles.

Sloshing in the rusty tub, reciting from Rimbaud's *Season In Hell,* she hears somebody on the other side humming, a wet gristled cough, glass breaking, cursing, more humming ... ("My whole burden is laid down. Let us contemplate undazed the extent of my innocence....*L'ennui n'est plus mon amour ...*"). Her teachers are always startled by her accent, how she gets the r's just right.

Using her toes to crank on more hot, rolling under colorless slippage, humming loud at whoever's drunk on the thin other side (his humming, mocked, cuts off). Stands, puts her wet back to him, takes the book, dripping, into a plain room where paint curls off the ceiling in flaggy beige pennants, reading aloud: "On highroads on winter nights, without roof, without clothes, without bread, a voice gripped my frozen heart: 'Weakness or strength, *faiblesse ou force,* there you are, it's strength. You do not know where you are going, nor why you are going; enter anywhere, reply to anything. They will no more kill you than if you were a corpse.' "

One lamp, one Bible beside the bed, and out the black sleeve of window, a parking lot. Three blocks away, star-blemished seawater, the dizzy froth of palms. Chilled, damp under the gray nubbled blanket and rough sheets, Phoenix writes in her green journal, a rapt, schoolish expression on her face.

In early lilac light, she pulls on her cut-offs, work shirt, hiking boots, reknots the leather headband. The hall, with its rug of floral burgundy, stinks of piss, booze, cigars. Hummer's door is part-open. She sees his bed in the center of a room bleak as hers, the floor bumpy with bottles.

In an aqua-tiled diner, Little Audrey's, the newspaper on the counter says Friday, October 5. She eats pancakes, head bent, deflecting stares. (You deliberately call attention to yourself and then suffer for it. Why? Why rebel if you are going to be miserably self-conscious? This was her mother, driving her to the therapist. Or was it her mother in the dressing room of the department store, seeing the lank red hair in her armpits, the brushy orange hair covering her pale legs, sinking down on the little dressing room chair, taking in her daughter's latest derailment from normalcy. Sighing. You could be such a pretty girl....Mothers always said that, observing their daughters with the regretful air of personally lost youth, plaintive, confusing beauty with simple youth, forming an impermeable jealous crisis between mothers and daughters.)

Phoenix shoves money under the plate, walks toward the wharf to use up her last connection to Venice Beach, the joint the guy who'd stolen her car had rolled for her, his thievish spit sealing the papers. She'd bought the car with most of her grandmother's birthday money. Now she has only a little left.

On sickly yellow sand next to the sidewalk, a man sleeps or lies dead under newspapers, a hump of kelp curled like a pet at his feet. A man with a waist-length beard, a peculiar armor of sauce pots and frying pans clanking off him, snaps caramel corn into a scatter of pigeons, all violet and green iridescence. Phoenix goes to the pier's end, stares down into rolls and glyphs of taupey-green, brine seeping into her mouth as she inhales, tasting his spit on wet, bitter paper. At its farthest edge, the ocean is purple with kelp, the middle teal with slatters of light, a squinting shine on the water, a coarse frieze of waves white with pockets of not-white, and at its edge, along cardboard-color sand, shell, dead bone, pocked stone, rock, humps of kelp like dogs, shiny dogs with pointy ears, feral faces. A seagull, speckled, lands in dream-like silence on a piling beside her, its body a kindergarten drawing, the legs sticking straight out from the middle of the belly. Her mother is a kindergarten teacher. Phoenix believes her mother didn't know what to do with her after age five.

Walking back up State, going past the bums hunched and drab, soft-knuckled against bright buildings. She can quit this, she's deliberately drifted out of the calm flat stream of college privilege; her poverty is transient, self-inflicted, romantic.

The Alpha Thrift Store has huge windows like movie screens, the icky amber of flypaper. She picks through musty, gnarly clothes, pouncing on the red circle skirt, gold dog-heads stamped all over it. She pays $1.25, but on the way out, spies a white nylon blouse, rhinestone buttons like doorknobs, a lasagna ruffle down the front, buys that too. On the sidewalk, she takes the clothes out of the wilted brown bag, stuffs them in her pack.

At a wrought iron table in a Spanish style courtyard with vine-covered shops, candle shop, linen shop, stationer's shop, cafe, she concentrates on the book she's borrowed from the university library. *The Tibetan Book of the Dead.* It tells the truth about dying, what dying's like, what happens after. She's prodded a stick of sandalwood incense into one of the perforated holes of the table. A cobalt-tiled fountain splashes like a tub beside her, pigeons queue on its swollen lip. Studying this *Book of the Dead,* her leg tick-tocks wildly; the whole idea of dying makes her hyper.

People stare at her. She's walked out of their rules, that's why. An exchange student from Benares told her that in India, you board a train, invent another name, you become untraceable. In India you can erase yourself, records there are so terrible. Here, license numbers, social security numbers, birth certificates,

8

school records, medical records, they nail you from the start. Her mother sent the Red Cross after her once, she's probably doing it again, this minute. Phoenix has a history of running away, beginning when she was eight, when her mother hurled her coloring books out the window in an attempt to clean the house. She had only come back because a scary man tried to lure her into his low green car. Her mother didn't believe her since Phoenix had this other history of lying, telling stories. But it was true. In fact, scary men were always trying to lure her into automobiles, which made it a crazy thing to be doing, hitchhiking.

She works morbidly through *The Tibetan Book of the Dead*, reading other people's underlinings: "If the disciple has learned, as the Bardo Thodol directs, to identify himself with the Eternal, the Dharma, the Imperishable Light within, then the fears of death are dissipated....this present universe is not the first and the last, but one of an infinite series without absolute beginning or end....At length the deceased passes out of the Bardo dreamworld into a new womb of flesh and blood, rising and rising again in the worlds of birth and death. Nothing is permanent but all is transitory." Phoenix memorizes this last line as ammunition against her family.

Heading back to the beach, Phoenix goes into a public restroom to change into the dog skirt and noodle blouse. Shovels in her pack until she finds the kohl; with her burnt face (heart-shaped, her sister pronounced, tracing Phoenix's face with a lipstick on the bathroom mirror) pushed up to the sheetmetal mirror, drags black powder inside her eye-rims. Rakes her hair (Florist's wire, her sister said, breathing hard, trying to make a French twist. My fingers are practically bleeding.) so it falls like coppery tentflaps from the beam of her part, undoes the top sparkly knob of the blouse so if she tilts out a ways, the tops of her freckly breasts show. Breezily naked under the red and yellow skirt, Phoenix sluffs, barefoot, to the theater.

Phoenix lets him take her to a black Volkswagen, its back seat ripped out, replaced with an avalanche of pornography. Roach clips knotted to a shoelace dangle from the mirror. She climbs in and fast food containers, styrofoam cups, cigarette wrappers, Buglers tobacco pouches crunch and squeak around her ankles. On the dashboard, a taupe-colored mouse worries a hamburger rind. She shrieks, it humps up, lurid pink eye fixed on her. She tries vaulting sideways from the car.

Hey there, hi there, ho there. Get a grip, dearie.

Deal snags the mouse by its tail, flips it in a tender arc toward the rear of the car.

Godot's impudent, a harmless, impotent rodent.

Deal's out of his burlap. White grease paint glimmers around his hairline, liner is caked around his eyes. He's wearing bellbottoms, a sheepskin jacket, and a poker player's hat, an oily band around its creamy dented surface, tilted back on his shoulder-length hair.

Why do you have those? She gestures to the sliding heaps of pornography.

I own a store.

Your own store? That's cool.

Yeah. The Dirty Bookstore. Once a month I go down to L.A. for fresh stacks of dirt.

Oh.

Does it make you uptight?

What?

Pornography.

I guess I don't understand it.

My best customers show up in rented trenchcoats, Dragnet hat brims pulled down over green, guilty faces, the old FBI trick, skulk in, collar up, hat down. Highest low profiles in the country, FBI agents and sex maniacs.

Maybe they're the same.

Deal pounds the plastic steering wheel. I like it. Oooh, I love it.

Deal's strapping worked me. The belt shooshing out the loops of his jeans, then he'd bounce it down my neck, shake it down my spine. This skinny shadow bending down (see him little, full of hair and little), taking down my pants, the crotch left v'd, to strap me. What worked was the thrill of putting up with an unusual experience most girls would not let themselves have.

To submit was observation, a way to control things, but the uniqueness of it broke down, novel depravity replaced by cool judgment. I wound up in a state of contempt, watching somebody arouse like that.

Though even now, a man's belt on a bed, half-slipping off the bed, gives me this quick puny shiver.

Deal tells her he was a child prodigy on weekly radio shows, the neighborhood whiz kid nobody would play with; brain-wise, he trounced everybody. He made three consecutive shaven and suited appearances on "College Bowl." Her parents watched "College Bowl" on Sundays, heron-legged TV trays circling the pondlike screen. He was probably one of the contestants she had been glumly made to witness. An uncalculated and astounding precocity to his parents, Deal had devolved into this present bewildering waste.

Some weeks after meeting him, Phoenix has dinner with these disappointed parents and a nine-year-old sister. Father, a bean-shaped psychologist, wears pouchy mole-toned cardigans; small of speech and eye, he seems repelled by human warmth. The family deferentially skirts his Lazy-Boy, the thin frequency surrounding him. Mother is a gamine, ginger-haired local actress who demonstrates for Phoenix how to uncurl cooked marrow from its collar of bone, thinning grayish paste over rye points, while contempt for her husband tightens her histrionic maroon mouth. Phoenix sleeps beside Deal in the family room on sticky red shag carpeting. By early morning, Mother is gone, chaperoning her daughter's field trip; Father is up, too, tunneling in drab sweater and slacks through the earth-tone corridors of the house. Phoenix is baffled by such intelligent, willfully inarticulate people, while Deal, in haste to leave, slams her index finger in the car door. He crushes aspirin for her to drink with rum, alchemizing pain into bearable drunkenness.

The second night, after the play, her arms wing up, a jewelry box ballerina's, as she spins. Deal mimics earnestly, without grace. (Phoenix took ten years of ballet, graduating to pearlescent toe slippers, when her rump suddenly blossomed and unbalanced her. Hormones, her mother's drear stab at solace.) They are in a cypress grove beside the ocean, a place where a lot of people drop mescaline, acid, peyote. A black twisty storybook wood, the sea's brackish air fraying through it.

The minute she stops her spinning to collapse on sand

lumped and pricking with black needles, he aligns his tiny weight on her. Fingers, sharp twigs, rasp up her blouse. Pressing against her, right away, he comes. She sees the black Florida-like mapping over his pants when he stands.

He helps her to her cold gritty feet, plants the poker player's hat on her head, his voice noncommital. Wanna head back? She doesn't remember if he knows her name.

She trips behind him on a sandy strip slimy with iodine-colored seaweed. Shale cliffs crook over them like stopped waves, inky water rinsing their feet.

Where do you live, she yelps.

Wherever's free.

They climb stairs from the beach, carry their shoes down blocks of uniform student housing, sparkly stucco apartments with slanting signatures like Tropicana, Sunrise, Fiji. Her teeth clank with cold, her bladder stings.

Deal goes into the back room of the headshop to find a used candle. The little shop smells of patchouli and hashish, its floor a tumorous swell of paisley and velvet pillows. The shelves have books on mysticism, astrology, witchcraft, numerology, herbal lore. She finds *The Egyptian Book of the Dead*. Deal returns and puts the sand candle on a bottom shelf, illuminating the second picture in two days of Meher Baba. Deal regards his stained pants with a complacent absence of embarrassment which repels her. Her bladder's killing.

Ah, where's the bathroom?

Deal points, hands her a satin cape with ivory lining, reeking of patchouli and something else. She pushes through glass bead curtains, finds the toilet and sink, reads the graffiti on the walls. A toothbrush sticks out of a mug on the sink, its bristles stomped like a shoe heel. There's no mirror, only a poster of W.C. Fields taped over the sink. She runs sink water as she pees, peeing noise embarrasses her. Her copper-red hair is wiry with sea salt. In a small mirror above the back of the toilet, her eyes stare back, roadstruck animals. Her nose is shiny, kohl leaking under one eye. She swipes at it, brushes sand off her cheeks and chin, yanks the string on the overhead light, heads back to the candle. Deal naked among the pillows, his eyes glassy, bland as an insect's, offers her a pipe which she declines.

He snores, riffling air like a newspaper, while Phoenix goes sliding out of the zipped-together sleeping bags. Holding the candle, she finds the back room, opens the tiny white door of a refrigerator, sucks fingerfuls of oily cashew butter from a jar labeled Sunshine Health Foods, swallows down some red wine. Dinner. A wettish briny odor clings inside the cape, while her mouth greedily works the grainy butter. She has no birthday money left.

What do I think? Maybe it's being brought down to a female animal, you know, not sexy, pissing, it's being an animal that can be caught, stuck there waiting for the piss to stop and you're vulnerable, exposed. Sex hides everything. They don't see you, they're busy in you, on you, all over you, but you're not what's there for them, you're this experience, feeling, not a person ... pissing, I don't know, I'd have to body-and-soul trust a man to piss in front of him and right now I can't imagine that, letting him hear, it's worse than intimate because in some way you're shamed, understand what I'm talking about, saying, huh?

At somebody's apartment, she's out of the shower first, arms raised, zipping up a child's white Sunday dress that stops at her knees, her legs burred with red-gold hair, auburn tufts sticking to damp underarms. Deal's still in the bathroom so she wanders around the apartment. Spindly emerald marijuana spiking from coffee cans and Baskin-Robbins barrels; the cottage-cheese textured walls slick and mossed as a terrarium. A friend of Deal's lives here, both of them enrolled in Russian Studies, but she's never seen Deal with one book going to one class. He's got keys to everything though, known ways to enter. Phoenix hangs out with him in stores that are closed, empty apartments, scrounging other people's food, bathing, sleeping. His Dirty Bookstore is a corridor with metal racks of magazines, a windowless cubicle with a shredding plaid couch and a metal cash box. She went in once.

She's steeping sassafras bark for tea when Deal finally comes out of the bathroom. In this florist's light, he's scoop-chested with a guppy sheen. He drags on his bellbottoms, they sit on the floor drinking rust-color tea from pottery cups. She trips out on his tiny hands, on their nicotine-orange tips, the nails concaved like strange ivory spoons. He lays out a tarot for her, scratching pearly crusts on his elbows, bringing up slow pricks of vermilion. He has wavy Victorian hair, girl's hair; his eyes are goatish, ashen green. His disproportionate head sits on a hairy physique; if he's not a prototypical dwarf, it's a close call.

The card backs are dimestore pink with slushy stripes of darker pink. Each card, in the middle, has a fuchsia rectangle with a white Rosicrucian Ankh. Deal, lotus-positioned, shuffles. Sitting across from him, Phoenix is supposed to be emptying her mind before cutting the deck three times, plopping the cuts back together. Deal lays out a ritual pattern, sixteen cards.

This, he intones, is where you are now
This is what covers you, protects
This crosses you, an obstacle
What happened in the past
What will happen

A condition you chose
A condition you will choose
Your home
Your highway
Your friend
Your foe
Your sword. Swords are strengths, sufferings
Your wand. Wands point to action, are generational
Your cup. Cups signify creativity, fulfillment
Your pentacle. Pentacles are wisdom, knowledge of the higher self.

The pictures terrify her. Her future is a red heart with three swords plunked through it, set against a drizzly background. Her protection is a lady in an orange tunic, tied up in gray strips, her eyes bound by gray, her figure circled by swords sticking in puddled dirt. Another card shows a giant's hand thrust out from an ominous cloud with Scilla around it; the hand cups a golden ball with a five-pointed star at its center. That card is her friend. Her foe is a fat greasy merchant, arms smugly x'ed before a golden horseshoe of goblets, a swollen cap on his head. Each card, as Deal turns it over, puts knickings up her spine. Ignorant of their subtler symbolic meanings, Phoenix translates doom, violent death, disaster, unnecessary revelation.

Deal is lecturing. The tarot manifests unconscious archetypes of Western civilization … blah and blah … he's on a major head trip while she's being kicked around by symbols … a phallic tower, lightning zapping a gold crown at its peak, a man and woman twirling like batons into nasty darkness. The only one she likes is the Empress, a pear-shaped woman planted among idyllic trees and Elysian streams; wearing a glittery crown, lofting a scepter, a Disney fairy dispensing false twinkly hints on sex, blood, death. Her mother, her mother's Ideal Mother.

* * *

Boy. I know why they call these things sewing machines.
Deal glances at her, his face a grinning wedge between his

17

chewed-up hat and his chewed-up sheepskin coat. Something about him is making her think of a city matron in furs, maybe the rich apostrophe of hair on his fleece collar. He reaches across, shinnying his hand up the little white Sunday dress. She tries not to block Reality-Flow, so she lets him. Suddenly she screeches, winds down the dusty window, half falls out of the car.

Stop a minute Deal. Stop the damn sewing machine.

Borrowing his cowboy boots, she stomps into the desert a few yards, yanks at lupine stalks, tugs up red hot pokers, stoops to seize an armload of pink wildflowers. Dry air pluffs like a bellows under her dress, threads between her legs with a hot, gauzy feel.

She galumphs back with the pilfered flowers. Deal is out of the car barefoot and peeing against a back tire while she stabs flowers into the visors, strews them along the dashboard, wraps red hot pokers around the steering wheel.

If she doesn't watch it, he makes her feel inferior, stupid. When he starts talking in Russian again, she'll fake sleep, it's her one defense. Genius can be a disability. Her eyes shut, feeling him snoodge the hat onto her head, tipping it so her face is in its satin shade. The unwashed maleness of his hair, his tobacco, boils around in that hat, a harsh, erotic smell. She naps until the jouncing of the car down gullied roads knocks her head against the window.

We're here, babushka. See that van over there?

Deal honey, I gotta pee.

The van, a corroded breadbox with a Confederate flag pouched in its window, leans on two wheels against a crumbly-looking shale cliff.

There be our friends, babushka. Pee quick so we can show our-selves to our brothers and sisters.

The sun slides like runny egg down a wall, sets so fast nobody pays attention. They sit around a small hot fire, mostly silent, passing bottles and joints. Up to now, she has been the quietest.

Question. What is the desert?

Deal, his friends, turn groggy heads to look at Phoenix. Except the girl with flat hair, her face pieced like a quilt, staring straight through her hand, held up to the fire.

Time's up. You guys are slow. You roll water back, roll it like carpet or linoleum, that's the desert. What's underneath.

One of them snorts, shakes his baffled head. I dunno Deal, you've found one spacey lady this time.

The ex-Vietnam guy looks at her with ferocity. He has a blond tonsure, a huge tattoo like a purple meat inspection stamp on his left bicep—One Hundred Years Lease Guaranteed Return.

What'd you say your last name was?

I don't have one.

Jesus, you look like somebody. I look at you and I see baby. B-A-B-Y. Know what I mean? Very unhandled. Why should people bullshit around with their life, man, it's a life.

The other girl stands, flicks a spark off her long skirt. Time to cut out.

The tonsure raises a hand. I'm bringing up an issue here.

Phoenix believes in Signs. Significance. Nothing is accidental. She will listen as if to an oracle.

Shit, I lost my fucking train of thought. He squats in front of her. Medals swing from a chain around his neck.

This trip is real, man.

What do you mean?

Shit. What do I mean. Don't hype me. You ever seen somebody iced? Dead?

No.

Whips your act together real quick. Or takes it to the ground. Depends which way you go.

Somebody threw dirt on the fire.

Hey, take it easy, she says.

He shrugs, swipes at his face. Yeah.

The van doors grind open, get dragged shut. She stays back. Deal says good-bye to his friends.

The van rocks, a tin loaf, over the unmarked road.

Deal?

What?

Can we let Godot go?

Out here? Liberate the mouse?

They open both doors, bug wings. The overhead light shines over the mess in the car, shriveling flowers. Crouched outside one door, she picks Godot off the backside of a *Hustler*, sets him on the headrest. He scrabbles down, flashes out of the car.

Wow. That's it.

I didn't have the heart to tell him he's had his last cheeseburger. No welfare in the desert.

Deal, he's better off free.

He's owl-meat.

They eat dinner at a truckstop.

Hey babushka, wanna be in a play?

I can't act.

Nothing to act. Just lie exceedingly still on the floor. Be the Dead Girl. Genet's *Deathwatch*.

Jeez, Deal, that's queer.

Not queer. Art.

Journeybook

Back home, love makes them jailers. The therapists, the psychologists, Mother hiring the Red Cross to search. Out here, no one cares. I am a Lens, people pour through me like water, water into my nothingness.

My journeybook. A hard green book with gilt edges, the gold rubbing off like those moth wings crushed between my fingers, the dark gold powder staining my child's white fingers. This is my secret self, anchor, the one reflection that might somewhat contain me.

Deal is dark-auraed, perverse, his brain immense, almost a monstrosity, his heart small and brittle, green as sticks.

Like those red and green painted Russian dolls my grandmother bought me, is the world illusion within smaller illusion, within smaller illusion, within smaller illusion down to the barely visible, scarcely touchable illusion?

People admire the Strong, submit to them, the Strong Ones suck the strength from this world.

I take no deliberate course, want no one to notice me, I discount what is Visible, look for what is buried, silently burgeoning. True.

For a moment I imagined them, my parents, in their blue car, looking.

In the coffeehouse, Deal shuffles solitaire, milking his scraggly beard, popping cards like waxed joints. Or in the pinball parlor, slamming puny hips into the machine, palming the flippers with monkey agility, tilting his pelvis against blue-orange flames until bells ding, lights scale in flashes. Fucking a gaudy machine.

He hunkers on a crate outside The Dirty Bookstore, challenging whoever walks by to a game of Go, regionally notorious for never losing. Food is a zero, he survives on drugs offered free. Meth endows him with prodigious asexual energy; Phoenix has seen him, on speed's baroque trajectory, recite Eliot's *Four Quartets*, most of *Lysistrata*, and a loosely strung, lewd rosary of Irish folksongs.

He's found a perfect Dead Girl, Deal tells the director, in a desert truckstop. Born for the part, he insists and is adamant; the director, meeting Phoenix, agrees.

Dead Girl runs errands, shifts light cues and gels, rearranges sets and props, fetches coffee from the machine, prompts from her script in the wings. Hook-and-eyed into a water-marked, stained bridedress and, like a browning lily, slipped into the grim singular vase of a rented coffin, to be photographed. The director also places her on humpy sand, ocean water spooning into her ears, whapping under her neck. The Dead Girl slides are blown onto a screen, grainy landscape behind the actors. A Giantess, arms like ivory pickets x-ing her acre of chest, Phoenix likes herself, not so much Dead as Enlarged, magnified by forgery.

Journeybook

To act, to be an imaginary other, is earnest Play. Yet assigned to one stifling character, being over-eager for some particular role, perhaps the way is lost. If one could locate the singular character, the singular speech that would truly free one ... Isn't the ideal to project beyond the self, the flesh a dense imprisoning, the personality a vicious confinement?

Rimbaud. I have known and lost him to time. He is the silver thread I balance and slip from, his precarious raw vision my own, his instinct mine, mine his, we agree, together, to seek the sublime through degradation, to pursue vision through experimentation.

With hot plate, kerosene lamp, and clothes in grocery bags, Deal sets a shoulder to the door. She's at his heels with macaroni and cheese boxes, powdered coffee, a twelve-pack of tamales, two bags of yellow cooking apples. It's November and maybe she'll do applesauce, borrow cinnamon, sugar, pots, from the people in the front house. Deal heads back to the VW for the space heater and sleeping bags while she sets out groceries, purchased with money from her job at the coffeehouse, next to the hot plate.

The toolshed sits inside a rotted fencing of gray-gold stubble. Past Isla Vista's student housing, down Storke Road and cutting an unmarked right onto a dirt path that hacks through a skinny eucalyptus thicket with a wild cumulus of red geranium, behind a funky white bungalow, a hundred yards or so behind that bungalow, is the toolshed she and Deal can have free. She explores its weak porch, plunks on a maroon armchair, the stuffing hard-panned into two corners, pluffing out the bottom.

Far out. I've attained poor white trash.

You are mah succulent white trash.

Shoot, don't spoil me, Deal.

They sit on their splintering porch, chomp tamales and apples in front of a nice, unpretentious sunset. She's decided against the applesauce, too involved. Marcia and J.B., who rent the front bungalow, attend the university, work nights at the same coffeehouse as Phoenix. They said she and Deal can use the bathroom, though Deal usually heads out behind the toolshed, and she does too, except when Marcia's old Plymouth is gone, then she bee-lines to their bathroom, washes her hair twice with Marcia's herbal shampoo, waltzing around the teensy bedroom while her hair dries, nosing a little through their stuff.

The L-shaped shed has a section like a boxcar, broad plank walls hung with farm tools. A concrete trough at one end barks out russet chunks of stinking water. A smaller room faces the opposite direction, a mattress shoved against one wall. Deal shakes out his sleeping bag, yellow ducks like winged bowling pins scatter over its blood flannel. The kerosene lamp stands on an upended crate, the hot plate plugs into the single outlet. The windows are opaque with web, she can vaguely see an expanse of white weeds going up to an auto salvage one direction, a Dairy Queen the other.

Frangipani incense sticking like darts in the wall above the mattress where Phoenix once in a while lies, rump upped like a bridge so Deal can crack his belt the way he's figured from his dumb magazines. She feels detachment. She is a lens. She has been so protected in this world, pinned by her parents to the bright side.

He got her the job at the coffeehouse, she works on nights he's rehearsing. He likes telling her about the production.

There's ten of us inside this maze of black panels. People walk through and bump into us reciting from Kafka's stories and letters.

Do your parts overlap?

Mechanical toys all drumming at once. I'm doing Kafka's *Letter to the Academy*.

In the mornings, she wears the sleeping bag like an animal skin, cueing Deal, holding the script while he paces, transforming himself into Kafka's talky ape.

When he comes into the coffeehouse with the other actors, she brings trays of food and cappuccino, wearing a lace dress from the thirties, lavender tights, black suede boots. The first time she balanced on Deal's knee, he didn't bother acknowledging her even as his hand snuck up her skirt. Her passivity, inspired by some curious poetic instinct, has begun to erode her.

Phoenix, Dreaming Death

Stepping backward, thumb out, preoccupied, busy seeing your future, not lights slowing behind you. You're cold though, and can't resist the block of heated air from the opened door.

Can't see the driver too well, even in the green dashboard glow. He has one of those knit watchcaps on, pulled down to the level of his glasses.

Where you headed?

South, far south as you're going.

I'm not going anywhere, just cruising.

Well, however far you're going.

He's glancing over, a strange, twitchy look. You know, you shouldn't be out by the side of the road, flaunting the fact you do whatever you damn please, being as you think society's all screwed up anyways.

You're staring at his hands rooted around the steering wheel, thick, white, gangly. His hands are monstrous.

Somebody might get the wrong impression.

One hand comes down, rests on the seat between you. When he lifts it, something glints, a silver revolver.

The gun, you mistake it for a toy. Toy gun, yeah.

He swerves the truck, without signaling, onto a road going into dark woods.

Your heart klunks crazily, falling, hitting a rib.

Ah, I'd like to get out now. Right here is fine.

He's speeding now, you can't jump without getting killed.

Sure. You can. I just need to check on something.

What? Your voice shrinks.

Thought maybe you'd be up for a little party.

You are falsely calm, even cheerful.

No, no thanks. I really wouldn't. In fact, I should get back to town. I mean you've got the wrong idea, really.

Now he's swerved up some darker road, more a dirt path, barely fitting his camper, the headlights sliding watery over tree trunks, branches scraping. Stops the truck.

A hollow thrumming, weird keening in your groin, expanding sweetish terror. You turn to this blurred figure, the breathing labored.

Yeah. Figured you and me could party some. Have ourselves a real good time back there, jerks his capped head toward the back. I've been told you hippie chicks fuck anything that moves. He talks, talks. I could come inside you, make you drink my come.

Blood dins in your head, a circular rushing, you can hardly hear anything.

I'm sorry, you have the wrong—

His fist cracks your cheekbone. Pain blows across your face, red August lilies, your childhood god can save you from this, if it be His Will to save you from this. Please don't let him hurt me, kill me. Please. I'm sorry. Oh please.

Shut up, don't you say nothing. And I'm not gonna kill you.

He wrenches you by one arm out of the truck, by your hair, your strong, good hair. Hauls you, legs thunking, up over the car fender, bumps you into the camper. The camper, a child's crayoned picture, two eye-windows, one mouth-door, no roof. Head skewed to one side, you see the little play-kitchen, the homely sheen of Formica, stainless steel, gingham curtains, a doll wife should be there, ironing while she watches TV.

You're punched backward onto a hard, small bed, your blouse shoved over your face.

Like I figured. Not much tits.

Puts his teeth on your icy nipples, your throat is astonished by its sound. Plugging inside you, that huge white hand, fist, the pain like the breasts', you are quiet then as he keeps punching through the blouse, shut the fuck up, bitch. Bitch.

You eat blackness, choke on blandly warm blood, head slammed and bent, sunflower against a muddied red field of bed, hissing of ocean, block of clean air over your belly, then hearing him at a drawer, shaking things, spoons, knives, forks, knives, spoons, your legs shake, tremble uncontrollably.

Like garbage, your homely unresisting weight is dumped out of the camper onto a blank witness spot of earth. Hear him above you, breathing, breathing, deciding. The gun goes off and you feel nothing but a sharp full ringing, violent tolling. You are clear as the truck goes off, you imagine red taillights wavering, compressed to sparks.

On a peculiar colorless rung of unconscious, you recognize faces along a white corridor, faces illumined with lurid orange and cobalt whorlings.

Your arms row the earth's needle sea, your legs are graceful choreography. Over flat red landscape, your ash and bone spray from the fiery Wheel, your brief life, flawless spark, caught between earth and an immense gold revolution of wheel.

She's on the last dryer load, has to be at the coffeehouse by five. Deal's in L.A. but not to buy magazines. Two FBI agents cruised by the bookstore, Deal's acid-tripping employee took set-up money, letting the little girl exit the store with a *Playboy*. They busted Deal; The Dirty Bookstore's shut down. Fine with her.

The washer lid's up, she's staring into lacy swish, thinking about dogs, maybe she'd like one. Isla Vista is overrun with Rin Tin Tin heads socketed onto assorted mutt torsos. Bandannas around their necks, skagging in slum-packs down the beach, most of them, named Cody or Grunt or Miso Soybean Rootbeer, trained to catch frisbees.

Dig this shit. The friggin washer's busted.

The economy-sized machine is chugging froth down itself and the floor. A slack-haired girl, hands on bony hips, glares.

So what's funny?

Phoenix can't quit even then, splurts Coke on her arm, laughing so hard. The machine keeps burping foam.

Shit. My old man's clothes are in there. Every one of 'em.

Then the skinny girl cackles, hoo, hoo. Both giggling, hauling cloudy armfuls to the street, swishing Babo over people, dogs, trashcans, car hoods, bicycles. When the machine groans, shudders to a halt, they open the door, poke their heads in its damp innocuous maw.

Ohwow. How much did you put in?

Shit. A few boxes I guess.

The girl plugs in her arm, brings out a flat mash of jeans, iridescent with soap.

You could do 'em over, in the regular machines.

I only had two dollars.

Bummer.

They panhandle, saying it's for thyroid surgery, a ticket to New York, for the deerskin dress with the purple cowrie shells at the leather shop. They get change when they wind up confessing it's for a laundry hassle.

In a Christmas tree lot next to the coffeehouse, Phoenix buys a spindly little fir for $3. After work, when a fraternity type picks her up, she clamps it in front of her face the whole time she's in his Mustang. If she's weird enough, he won't bother her.

Next morning she walks across the rattly dry field to the convenience store for cranberries, popcorn, kite string. On the porch with Marcia's bulb-eyed dog, threading corn and cranberries, she and the dog snarf a lot of popcorn. Looping strands around the scrawny tree, pinching its trunk between Deal's coffee-table book on sexual positions and her *Book of the Dead* to hide the window, Deal's socks stuffed into two broken panes.

In the night, she feels skitterings across her legs, hears subtle persistent noise by the tree. By daylight, she sees the string chewed, sagging empty off the branches. Mice.

Deal returns to the toolshed on foot. The Volks was impounded, they'll have to hitch into Isla Vista or get rides in the Plymouth.

Deal's Kafka show is going, his voice shot to hoarse ribbons at the end of every performance when he asks, every night, was he *good?* She thinks he *acts*, hangs on top of words like rafts, keeps a stiff balance with logic, theories, verses, speeches, rules of play. His acting is memorized, clever, an artist would not use a net the way Deal does. He paces the false cage, shouts the rote paragraph, squats, regards people in an eerie mime of apes locked in zoos, eyes urgent, fathomless, dumb.

The ape's fate, to be gawked at, misunderstood, is Deal's reward.

Striving for compassion, she says he was good.

Journeybook

Christmas. I feel indistinct enough to vanish. Last week I called my grandparents, they sent money, and I said I was busy with exams. Last night I was alone, pretending it was not Christmas Eve, then knowing it was and pretending it didn't matter. No friends. No family. No one. I chose this, asked for this, wanted to strip myself of habit and season, the deeply consoling architecture of love. Will I not be released, by sacrificing everything? The prisoner who has nothing, the saint who lets go the world, these approach the Eternal, the harsh grace of solitude. My journeybook, these pages, transform, transmute, the alchemical Key. Without language the silence is untranslatable, unendurable. Quiet, motionless as possible, I am still so deeply attached to this world. I render experience into stubborn inhibited language. Stupid notes. My presumed intelligence, so vaunted in schools, in classrooms, a vain banner shielding me from faces, things. I want to serve the essential, elusive experiment. I want to have the curiosity of a God without judgment.

I am not beautiful or monstrous. I want to forget what is smugly known, complacently taught.

In the coffeehouse, by one a.m., the fluorescent lights are on, and the black plastic chairs look like crookedy-legged insects. Cockroaches. The round tables have pressed pieces of something vomity-looking dipped in thick, clear acrylic. The short walls are rotten, water-stained, the orange rug balding and greasy. Bessie Smith's "Kitchen Man" scratches on, the needle wadded in lint. Phoenix is going around huh-ing out candles in their plastic-netted red glasses, then wiping salt and peppers with a gray grody rag. Half an hour ago, this place was exotic, candlelit, espresso-smelling. Now it's a dingy room in slushy light. Exhausted, she plugs in the vacuum, angles it listlessly around the ugly furniture, whumps something huddled under a table by the little plywood stage.

Jeez, what's this? J.B.?

J.B. is behind the bar washing glasses and cleaning the espresso maker.

I think Gilbert and Leah forgot their little kid.

Marcia answers from behind the cash register. No, he's crashing with us, favor for Leah.

He's a cute little kid. Don't you feel sorry for him?

Not really. He's cool. Gilbert's convinced he's a genius. He says Einstein and Schweitzer never talked as kids either.

Gilbert, the owner of the coffeehouse, pouts like a silent screen star burdened with charisma while his wife, Leah, runs the place at a profitable clip around him. He composes elliptical spirit-dramas, staging them in the dirt lot next door. Unplanned characters jump on and off stage, intended ones appear sporadically. Gilbert, center stage, arms out like crossties, eyes rolling in their sockets, enacts soul maladies while his actors, also his waitresses and cooks, fumble the script, hatchet lines, pocket crumbly joints and sticky pills flipped onstage by a tripping audience of dogs and people.

Ogress with orange teeth, an explosive voice, and a nosy, melancholic disposition, Leah trawls around the dim coffeehouse in spangly skirts, her skin jaundiced like her teeth, hair nailed in one dark horsy plug down her broad back, eyes the chlorine green of a Weimaraner's, devouring her workers who give grist to her appetites. She sleeps with all the men, a few of the women, gulps them whole, increasing the oily bulk of her Bad-Mother presence. Everyone, naive and diddle-daddling, gets towed under Leah's smoky, spittled skirts. While waitresses and cooks prop up Gilbert's megalomania, Leah dangles them from her Long Sallow Tit.

Phoenix sees their nameless son, in a red t-shirt, bare ass hunkered in the doorway of the coffeehouse, dirt-streaked, his small-square hands dreaming over an old yellow truck, noon sun nearly obliterating his quiet figure.

Hey, pretty neat truck.

He isn't playing with the truck, he is only anchored in some way to it.

There are no children in Isla Vista. Her hand hitches, caught in his dirt-toughened hair. Maybe it's ok, ok not to be played with or talked to or called by name. (Hell, he can pick a name when he grows up, Leah says. Everybody hates their name, I'm doing him a favor.) And maybe he is a genius. Still, Phoenix thinks he's neglected, however benignly.

She keeps to the periphery of these people who switch partners like hot potatoes. While she's there, the fortuneteller splits from a waitress, Cinnamon, who's picked up by the main cook. A yawn and shift of tribal limbs, everyone in one vast wicked bed. She hears several versions of how Cinnamon was in a Synanon treatment center and Gilbert snuck her out, but she split from him to be with the fortuneteller, and how these two proceeded to fry themselves on speed, now the cook's getting her beautiful again, maybe pregnant. They live in a cottage on Storke Road, near Gilbert and Leah, down the road from Marcia and J.B., and behind them, Deal and Phoenix. She can tell Cinnamon's house

33

from the road by the glinting of grocery carts, like piled jacks, on the porch.

Phoenix likes the fortuneteller. He is small like Deal and has a pocked, androgynous face, eyes feline with kohl, a gold hoop in one ear, a ruby stud in one nostril. He lives in the coffeehouse day and night, wearing a renaissance shirt, brocade vest, bell-bottoms, and black ankle boots, his sneaky fingers concealed in rings. He is full of sly compressed sensuality, an arcane sexuality irresistible to college girls, who stand in line to be taken into his purple booth where violet symbols, stitched by Cinnamon's chemically flying fingers, glow against black velvet pillows. They shiver at the long filthy fingernails, the sweet oily voice reading a dollar's worth of their minds.

J.B. and Marcia provide dull ballast, J.B. an economics major with a headband around his hopelessly straight head, Marcia, her face in a lethargic slope, the features struggling to lift off the flat inert surface, utterly bland; she looks and acts like a plumped couch of sprawled breasts, splayed hips, jutting rear. She has "things" as she calls sex, with whoever … including Deal, she confesses to Phoenix with additional blandness. Now she's doing a living "thing" with J.B. She enjoys telling everyone her father is a Baptist minister in Iowa.

Phoenix waits on the tables, eats free food, rolls the vacuum around, but what money she gets, Deal seems to spend. The toolshed is damp and mildewed, the wintry coastal season weights their sleeping bags with cold fog. When she gets sick, feverish, Deal hauls their stuff out to the '52 Cadillac she bought with Christmas money from her grandmother and chauffeurs her to a commune down in Santa Barbara.

Journeybook

Sickness, welcome disordering of the senses, this fever. Invoking truth and ignorance, not knowing what will come, as in dreams. I will turn back, one hand brimming with white pictures, the other a black torrent of images. Perhaps this journey of mine is terrible indulgence, running away a subtle obstacle. I am inordinately attached to solitude and terrified of being an Artist, Artist of what? Language? I float down my journeybook, down these pages, a raft in brilliant murky waters.

Find a cabin in the forest, seal up its doors and windows, never come out. Be one step braver than Thoreau.

Oh, Deal, yuck. Why does it have to look like mayonnaise?

So I can win best Kraft salad.

Then we need to roll you around in tinted marshmallows and fruit cocktail.

She's on their mattress in the salmon-colored room watching Deal slather his legs and arms with cortisone cream. His psoriasis crusts and oozes like battery acid, whitish patches cover his ears and hands. He extends one arm, waiting. Since she's known him, they've done this twice. She tears a length of sticky saran from the box, winding it around and around the arm. Wraps the other arm, kneels to wrap his thighs, calves. Sealing up hairy afflicted flesh feels more intimate to her than sex. Part nurse, part embalmer, she feels tender, repulsed.

I feel like a goddamn fruit basket. Would you go out to the front room and get my cigarettes? They're in my jacket.

Should you smoke? I mean won't saran wrap catch on fire or something?

Who gives a flying fuck.

Crackling like groceries in his plastic wrap, Deal takes the lit cigarette in his mouth with a wince of humiliation.

Two nights before, he'd had a migraine, crisscrossing the commune's green kitchen in mad wired strides, his hands gripping his head, hair poking in brutal spurts between his fingers. Calmly, she'd swept and remeasured the lapsang souchong he'd knocked across the wood counter. She was adjusting blue flame under the pan of water when he'd started slamming his forehead into the door frame. She went over but he shoved her. She'd given up and gone to their room, hearing the dull percussion, his head duh-duh-duh, on the wall.

In the morning, he opened their door, a dish towel draped over one arm, a glass of orange juice on a white plate in his hand, bowing elegantly. Deal was brilliant, yet he embarrassed her. Painters, musicians, poets lived in this house, his intelligence seemed dowdy. Each morning, someone taped a haiku in the shower stall, ink smearing and running, words dissolving. Phoenix understood this was Art, but Deal had to point out the disadvantage to late risers—that by the time he gets the shower there's black sludge on the floor staining the soles of his feet. He humiliates her with discordant remarks, talks too loud and too much, fastened to feverish logic, the clever uncle you once adored, embarrassing you in front of friends.

Her first night, Phoenix feels well enough to climb off her mattress and talk to Semi in the kitchen. Semi cooks for whoever wants food. Short-grain brown rice with curry or soy sauce, feta cheese with steamed vegetables. Promiscuous in the kitchen, she is stubbornly faithful to the shower poet.

It's true. Every November, since I was sixteen, I get superficially suicidal.

Superficially? How can anybody be superficially suicidal?

Because it's more mood than intent. Shedding leaves. It goes away.

Semi's dun-colored hair flops past her butt. She has a batik scarf tied around her head, earrings like Tibetan temples. Her spiritual dharma, she solemnly tells Phoenix, is to clean up after the poet's psychic and physical garbage, to experience neither resentment or pain. Like Huxley's Goddess behind the Genius. Right now she's pressed to her limit of garbage collecting, having to share him with a loud blonde Australian, both of them pregnant.

When she passes the darkened bedroom on her way to the bathroom, Phoenix just sees blank walls and stacks of poetry rising like termite mounds from the floor. She wonders how the three of them sleep together, who is next to who.

No esoteric philosophy, not even a schedule of chores binds the commune. If everybody stays in tune, everything evolves. If the food's spoiled, the rent's late, and the landlord's pissed, somebody went and brought bad karma on the house. If people hoard food in their rooms, that promotes bad energy. Semi, earth mother, steaming her monotonous rice and vegetables, her martyred devotion to the poet, is the closest thing to a business manager. When she makes chapatis with ghee, people come out of the walls, chopsticks litter the sink. The old stucco bungalow with its dank warren of rooms smells of woodsmoke, incense, scented candles, soy sauce, curry, and, in the bathroom, Dr. Bronner's. Everyone shares the blue-and-white gallon jug of Dr. Bronner's lung-scalding peppermint soap. A stink of puppy shit begins to permeate the house after someone brings a skittery yiping litter into the newspapered hallway. Semi plants gentle protests on toothpicks into the poops, paper masts on mushy brown vessels. Her gentleness works. The puppies are removed to the yard.

Phoenix isn't sure why, but now, when she looks at Deal, she sees Pulp. When he straps her, her inside eye sees Pulp. He is at the theater every night, they've used up what money she'd earned at the coffeehouse. After the forty-dollar deposit to the landlord, their share of the commune's rent is still unpaid. Deal's legendary charm, in this house, has no charm. The Cadillac broke the first week; it crouches, rabbit-haunched, in a parking lot off Lower State until somebody has money for a fuel pump.

No problem for Deal. He will pare his needs to nothing. Panhandling, scrounging for meals, bumming cigarettes. She's left worrying about the car, the rent, being the source of fraying communal spirit.

On the night she's already thinking of leaving what is no longer a very good thing, Phoenix sits up in bed, her hair wet and Bronner-fragrant. Deal comes in, sits on the mattress edge. Something feels, to her, out of whack.

Why, she asks, propped on one elbow, does this room feel so weird?

He has a pinched doggish look. Guilt. She feels awake as cold water.

He was at the cast party, that's why he's late … yeah, he met someone there, nobody really, the costumer's assistant, she'd helped him backstage … Yeahsure, they spent a little time together at the party … Well yeah, they did play around some, hell, could he help it, there's always excitement at the end of a show. Anyway it was her idea, she was coming onto him, could he help it he was one of the stars … yeah maybe his ego did get blown up a little … Ok so, so he balled her. No big deal. She wanted him to. It was nothing. A favor. He was home now, wasn't he? That proved something.

Free to rail, to slam down grievance after grievance. Faults he admits with a hands-up defenselessness that crazes her. She stalks over, flips on the overhead light, from its severity comes a sound harder, wilder than hers, gutting him, backing him in a corner, his hands over his ears, a puling monkey. A voice that flogs, weeps, lays crimes on his doorstep.

Look. You knocked me around with your belt, with your perverse little gig. I don't need it, man. I don't need any of it. Who the hell needs somebody like you?

Her voice, hers now, and quiet, shakes.

Keep the car, Deal. Go live in it, like that little rat you had. Like Godot. Cars are bad luck for me anyway. Goddammit. I don't even know what to say. People like you are just so disappointing.

Journeybook

There was this man, a hairy little man, he kept an accordion, pleating it in and out, in and out, making awful sounds. The accordion was me. Blown out, shoved in, making these sounds. Nothing to do with mescaline, acid, any of that. I knew I'd be the type to fly out a window howling I was a ghost, embarrass myself in some smash-up, newspaper death.

My Rimbaud, little soul of mortification, inverted ascetic, penitent of miniature indulgence, saint of passive debauch ... I am in the world to abandon safety for truth, to vow valuelessness so I may see Perfect Value ... This is my Art, its companions perpetual cowardice and shame.

I do not need the accordion player anymore. I can be alone, soundless.

Phoenix crosses the footbridge above the highway, floating over cars like fog, drops her pack on a flowering slope of iceplant. She believes in avoiding big cars, the ones like bank vaults with tinted windows, the drivers with sunglasses and tight cheesy smiles.

She's waving off a VW van when this homey old truck chugs up, practically nipping her bare heels. It has a polished tomato snout and a homemade wood camper. A guy in dimestore shades leans his head out the passenger window. He has a tight cheesy smile.

Hi.

Hi. You headed south?

Anaheim.

Disneyland?

Yeah, if you're Snow White.

She hugs the passenger door of the cab, feet glommed to her pack, wary, ready to haul ass if her instincts are off, if these guys get the least weird. The one nearest her, the cheesy one, has a Budweiser clamped between his thighs. His jeans are brand new, starched, his white shirt's got knife creases from just coming out of the package. His hair's billiard-short, his eyes slew like a tough guy's, his mouth grudgy.

Hey Snow White. I don't buy that you're Snow White. I think you're a witch. I mean no chick stands around on freeways in a black cape unless she's a witch.

The other guy hitches up on the steering wheel to stare at her better.

What Hap's saying is he digs you in that cape. He pointed his beercan at you so I stopped.

Oh great, she smiles, jittery, looks out the window.

My name's Ron. You've already had the questionable pleasure of meeting him.

Ron is handsome, which illogically reassures her.

I like how you drive. Most guys speed.

Yup, our boy Ron keeps his belly to the road, inching it like a damn farmer.

And we're alive, right Hap?

Hap belches, squints at her. His eyes, both expression and color, are hard, sapphire.

Your real name's what?

Phoenix.

Yoo-nique. Far fucking out. Witch name.

The idea of being a witch is appealing. She lets her hold off the door a bit.

When they stop at a Bob's Big Boy, Ron tells her he rents warehouse space in Santa Barbara, builds lutes. Renaissance and Baroque lutes. He sells one a month to a shop in Anaheim. He also plays flamenco guitar. Hap would smoke a million cigarettes before he would bother to reveal anything about himself.

Phoenix says she's an actress, that she quit reading tarot cards because of other people's emotional expectations, that she's thinking of keeping quiet a whole year as a spiritual experiment. Hap says that's easy. Harder to keep yakking for a year. Her lies acquire luster, a credible gleam, as she tells them. She eats tons, hoping they'll pay. They do.

Outside L.A., Ron pulls off the road. He and Hap vault a barbed fence, go sit on the edge of a weedy cliff. She slides down a sand dune, runs up to her hips in loud cobalt waves, her skirt bunched at her waist. When she trudges back up, legs stinging with salt, Ron's stretched on his face, asleep. Hap's grinding a cigarette under his boot heel, ignoring her.

You guys mind if I crash in back until we get there?

Suit yourself.

The camper smells of fuel, plywood, stashed moldy clothes. Two shelflike bunks are heaped with old thin sleeping bags. Clothes, books, and records are everywhere. *Siddhartha. In Watermelon Sugar. Damien.* Dylan's "Blonde on Blonde" album, Frank Zappa's "Weasels Rip My Flesh," a bunch of Ravi Shankar. An odd-shaped plywood crate, probably a lute. A guitar case.

Through an opening into the cab, wood beads strung along it, Phoenix stares beyond the soft chucking of beads awhile, then lies down in the emptiest place. Like flood water, the highway blurs, rising gray under her.

Tweedy shit, Hap says, scuffing his boot against a bright plaster dwarf. The dwarf, on the flagstone entry, points emphatically toward the door, which Ron opens with one hand, carrying in the wood crate with the other.

Phoenix trails into the music shop, grubby, feeling herself shrink, a thing which keeps happening. Wishing she was still asleep in the truck as the shop owner crosses the shimmering oak floor, her haughty cheek brushing Ron's, eyes blinking, snaky, over Hap and Phoenix. Doll-sized, sun-faded, with lank, grayish red hair curbed off her forehead by yellow satin ribbon.

Someone practices a harp in the back; a flurry of notes ices up around them. The shop is lit by ivied, leaded windows; Renaissance instruments hang on pegs along parchment color walls.

Ah, Ron, delighted. Another perfect instrument, I hope?

Ron kneels to unlatch the cedar-lined crate, lifts an instrument like a cleft pear with a handle; at its smooth center, roses twine, ornately carved. The pegs squeak as he twists them, thumbs the double strings, tunes the lute. He offers it to the owner who conveys it with overblown pomp to a bench. Her spread-kneed, immodest pose mocks the prissed uptilt of her chin. Giving an airy smile, she plucks the silver- and brass-wound strings.

Gorgeous bass, Ron. Better even than the last. Edward will be tickled. Your craftsmanship is more remarkable with each instrument. If you'll come back to the office, we'll get your money Could you possibly have another in six weeks' time? My waiting list keeps growing.

Phoenix and Hap slunker over by the bulletin board, read calligraphied notices for Renaissance Faires, lute and vihuela concerts, Elizabethan banquets, costume rental shops. Hap looks mongrel-mouthed, waiting for meaty tatters of bone.

That bitch thinks she shits pearls.

Shh. Maybe she's more evolved than you are.

Yeah, right. Broads like her annoy the hell out of me.

Why?

44

Golden teaspoons up their asses.

She likes Ron, that's obvious.

Hap grunts, shoves his hands down his back pockets, lifts up on his heels, loudly farts.

Ron emerges, rosy with cash. Hap and Phoenix perk up and are out the door, its temple bells dingle-linging before Ron's done talking.

Yee-up! Hap two-steps into the street, dodges a honking car.

Aren't you overdoing this? Hippies are supposed to be non-material.

Hell, I'm tired of being hungry. And who's a hippy? I hate hippies.

Ron appears, grinning paternally and shoving a fat bundle of cash down one boot. Who wants food?

In a harvest gold booth at Denny's, they're slumped around redwood tailings of ribs, a swampy goo of sundaes. Hap belches. Better check on my old man.

Your parents live in L.A.?

My dad's in Newport.

Ron casually unpeels a twenty, lets it float onto his plate. I'll make some calls there. Let's split.

Since the music shop, Phoenix feel her ego leaking out, a physical sensation, a soul-hemorrhage. By the time Ron takes her arm, pulling her into a head shop, she's already gone, invisible.

Hap sulks on the curb. When they come out, Phoenix has on a new Indian-embroidered shirt. Ron grins down at Hap. Ready?

Still pussy-whipped ain't you? Hap's answer is snarly.

They drive for what feels like a whole chain-linking of hot afternoons through suburb after suburb, slowing down in one with low stubbed houses, balding lawns, junked cars. Ron parks in the driveway of a gum-pink bungalow. Hap gets out, then sticks his head back in the window.

I'll see (a) if he's home, (b) if he's plastered.

A minute later, he's flagging them from the doorway.

Mr. Simmons, tamped into a rust recliner in front of his TV, wearing boxer shorts with gold coins on them … his hairy arms purple with tattoos. He is a tuna fisherman; Hap said he and his brother spent summers either on the boat or mending nets in the driveway. Tuna-stinking June through August. Right after Hap's mother died, his brother turned MIA on a helicopter mission over Laos. Leaving Hap—you goddamn yellow pukin' bum, his father bellowed at him one night, full-throttle on booze. After which, as Hap told it, he'd started sobbing, saying how it was just the two of them. Hap cleared out.

Hi there, Mr. Simmons, long time no see.

Long time yourself. He launches belly up from the recliner to grip Ron's hand.

Mr. Simmons stares until Hap catches on. Whoops, sorry, Pops. A friend. Phoenix, I'd like you to meet my father, Roy Simmons. Dad, this is Phoenix.

Goddamn kooky names you kids go by.

They shake hands. If ah, if Mrs. Simmons were here, you two gals …

There is a brief loss of momentum.

Hell, come on back to the kitchen, I'll fry us a mess of egg sandwiches. I was about to fix a couple myself.

The eggs are ruffled with blackened butter, the bread tastes like salted angel cake. Mr. Simmons and Hap wolf down three apiece, a bit of yolk stuck in a fold of Mr. Simmons' lower lip. The meal boosts his spirits, or maybe having company, having Hap home, even if he wasn't the one with the guts to disappear over Laos. Ron and Phoenix poke at their sandwiches with dulled appetite.

Mr. Simmons' heart is slapped to mud, anyone can tell that. Politeness works on him like a narcotic, so Hap is meek, calling him sir, speaking respectfully. It gives her a place, something to do, so Phoenix clears dishes, knots on an apron she finds in the

46

cupboard under the sink. Inside the yellow rickrack pocket is Kleenex, lipstick smudges on it.

Ron's talking on the living room phone while Hap and his dad take clumsy pokes at conversation. Their efforts make Phoenix think of card houses, when one impatient calculation, one bum card, blows the total architecture. She gives them privacy plus the comfort of noise, clanking dishes and pans under running water.

Then Ron's leaning in the kitchen doorway, so handsome she nearly can't look at him.

There's a party up in the canyon, anybody want to go?

Yeahsure. Hey Pops, mind if we shove off for a bit? Would that be all right, sir?

Oh sure. Kids gotta be on the move, always think they're missing out. Go on. Have fun.

Down the hall she finds a dark mildewy bathroom, splashes water on her face, sniffs her oniony armpits, swings open the medicine chest, rubs on somebody's Old Spice deodorant.

The ripped leather in the cab boils the backs of her thighs. Ron navigates the tarnished linkage of freeways while he and Hap discuss the rich chick, Naila, who throws incredible parties when her parents are out of town, parties that go on for days. Ron went to one and stayed two weeks. She's juiced on speed half the time, Ron says. Which is why he left. In the canyon, the truck labors up woodsy serpentine roads.

A little decadent, mutters Hap, looking around.

Ron laughs. You'd get used to it.

Naila whips open both carved front doors. Behind her, the living room rises, a pale, immaculate vase, the field of glass behind it revealing an oblong turquoise stone in the ground, a pool.

GOD AWMIGHTY. WHERE HAVE *YOU* BEEN?

Ron, twitchy, embarrassed, introduces Phoenix and Hap. Naila smiles glossily, blonde hair tapping her bare waist, a fuchsia bikini molded to her whitish saltine skin. Starved to near perfection, Ron had joked in the truck.

Like the sinking half of a double date, Hap and Phoenix lag behind Naila and Ron.

Which way to the bad beer and good dope? Phoenix yelps, cloddish in her Indian blouse and shredded jeans, hoping to have an ok time.

Wealth and poverty are an illusion. His voice is wheezy, self-important. There is no difference between money and a heap of shit.

Jeez, I don't know. Phoenix feels claustrophobic. Like everyone else at the party, they are wasted. At the shadowy curb of the pool, thunking water with their feet, ladling little plugs of poolwater up and down. Wobbly mosaics float around the pool lights, aqua and soft black geometry.

Have you read Baba Ram Dass?

Maybe. I might have.

He was Tim Leary's partner. He's off drugs now, totally into the spiritual. He says most of us …

But they're both watching this girl, Giacometti-limbed, naked, gleaming on the lip of the diving board, raising arms in a steeple and toppling in, surfacing, stroking to the shallow end, gliding up the curved steps, dripping light-filled water toward the house.

… he says we're trapped in bodies, flies in the bottoms of jars. Oh God. Her body is God's.

Yeah, she's a trip. Phoenix had seen her earlier, cruising the living room wearing only blue and purple beads in her gold Brillo of pubic hair.

Phoenix pads across a gray flank of the patio, her feet drying on its still-warm cement. Asks where the kitchen is. Her head feels spacey from hashish and beer. Food. Poke things into the hole in the middle of her face. Food maybe.

Whaddayasay sportsfans. Parked against a stainless steel, restaurant-sized refrigerator, in a kitchen the size of most people's houses, are Ron and Hap. Hustling girls. Jeez. Little girls.

Hey, peel yourselves off a minute.

Say please, Hap grins, moving himself off the refrigerator, re-attaching to a marble countertop.

Introduce me, someone, to these *enfants terrible*?

The girls giggle. Couldn't be over thirteen, blue shadow gorping up their baby eyes, faces glowy with crib sweat. Actually, Phoenix observes, teething a hunk of cheddar, they're tripping on Ron, freaking over the long blond hair, the gorgeous face. Poor Hap. Sideline material. She finds a knife to dice cheese, mincing itsier cheeses, making cheese disappear, wondering if Hap minds his friend always getting first pick.

The volume on "Cheap Thrills" goes skyhigh, everybody in the kitchen wails with Janis … "jes like a baaaalaalaall ball and chayaayain...."

Hap's hanging over her like a banana skin.

Whatcha doing?

Making cheese do stuff.

What stuff?

All kinds.

Hey. I kinda liked the way you moved around, kind of dancin', on the beach the other day.

Gee thanks. I kinda like, you know, the way you pound down a beer.

Shit. I can't stand cynical bitches.

So?

So yourself, bitch.

She locates what has to be rich Naila's room. Funny, it resembles her own. White and gold curlicue furniture, expensive dolls on shelves, Persian kitten and palomino posters, a *Desiderata* scroll. Knowing better, Phoenix rolls back the closet doors, bites her lip at the sight of so many clothes—batiked, tie-dyed shirts, suede vests, halter tops, miniskirts, a fringed leather jacket, lace and paisley, feathers, beads, leather hats, scarves, boots, moccasins, sandals … an entire boutique. Phoenix takes the batik shirt, silver-button Indian moccasins. She's busy wadding up a skirt to stick under her blouse when the bedroom door clicks open and Ron lurches in, his arm circling one of the kitchen babies.

Oops.

Hithere, says Phoenix bright as a dime, stuffing the skirt, snitching the moccasins. I'm outa here, you guys go ahead, feel free, do whatever.

The girl giggles. Ron's moving like a jellyfish. Phoenix almost feels for her, being that dumb-virgin.

She finds her way to the front doors, to the red truck at the end of the driveway. Hap's flopped across the hood.

Hap?

Yeah what.

What're you doing?

What're you doing? he mimics.

People are crashing like fruitflies in there.

What's new. Parties do that to people. People do that at parties. Whatever. It's supposed to be fun. Why? You wanna cut out?

Where?

My old man's place.

What about Ron?

I wouldn't concern myself.

The truck coasts like a toy down the steep hills. In the cab, they sit way apart. Alone with Hap is worse than being alone. There's no small talk, and all sorts of repressed violence hangs around him. He looks like a fist keeps regularly popping him between the shoulder blades. When he bothers to talk, it's in jabs, feints, whatever it takes to keep people off. Sometimes she's towed into his violence, gets weird urges to punch or kick. The other day they'd started rolling around, wrestling. He'd hit her hard, now she has a big, grapefruit-colored bruise on the inside of one thigh. He'd laughed at it, at her.

What happened to that other girl, the one you were sort of talking to?

Hap snorts. Jailbait. Ron's got no self-discipline.

50

They cruise past all the mansions, a necklace of softly lit temples. A muggy tension in the cab, having to do with their being alone yet repelled by one another.

Before they're even in the house, a dull pink cube in street light, they hear Hap's father snoring down one end of the hallway.

You go ahead, crash in my room, it's the one opposite my old man's. I don't go in there anymore.

She uses the bathroom, finds his room, flips on the light. This isn't Hap's room. Twin beds with navy corduroy bedspreads, twin desks with gooseneck lamps. Twin everything. On one of the desks, a framed color photograph of Hap's brother, kind of a beefier, dumber version of Hap. Or just a bad picture. People take bad pictures all the time. Because he's dead, or at very least missing, she makes an excuse for the picture. She sits on one of the beds, wondering if he'll come in, change his mind. To have somebody, even Hap, would help.

Journeybook

There is God to be found, abandoning the familiar. Terrorized by self-betrayal, I think of suicide. Killing myself would be stupid, inartistic, succumbing to the crumbling edge of the highest cliff. A final Peace, dropping with unshakable, palpable optimism, knowing God is on the other side. I like wanting God, the worst thing would be to let go of this one belief. I am not free at all, I am bound to faith. What did she say, brave Anne Frank, I still believe people are really good at heart. I must believe this of myself, that I deserve life even as I let go.

Outside the zoo entrance, Ron plays flamenco guitar music, the case open at his feet, its sapphire lining glittery with quarters, dimes, nickels. Phoenix is stretched belly-down in the grass, reading a book of poetry. Hap's somewhere in the zoo with Ron's sister, Margaret, and Margaret's daughter, WeeBee. Hap will have to push Margaret's wheelchair up to the rails so she can see better.

They drove to San Diego to visit Margaret, her house in a subdivision so new, trees spike like broomsticks out of emerald plots of rigid sod. Monopoly houses, three variations of ranch style alternate up and down the cul-de-sac; the whole street could be featured on a bag of lawn fertilizer except for Ron's truck, a nasty, red blight parked in front of Al and Margaret's brand new home. Three hippies sashaying barefoot into their house, tracking dirt and dope, drawing stares from neighbors, none of this suits Al's nerves, snappish to start with.

Margaret's face is Ron's twin in its unequivocal beauty, right down to the rich long mouth and even teeth. This loveliness stops at the neck, vanishes into Margaret's unfortunate casing of fat— making Phoenix think of a deboned chicken breast zipped into a pink housecoat, plonked in a wheelchair. WeeBee, the six-year-old, is a physical ringer for Al, which, unfairly, makes her difficult to like.

Ron sits on the grass beside Phoenix, taking a break. She notices how girls fixate on him, instantly helpless. What could it be like, to be effortlessly desired? Phoenix once sat on cold tile before the mirror on the back of her mother's bathroom door, determined to accept whether or not she was pretty. She was, she wasn't, she was, wasn't. What was pretty? She gave up.

What's wrong with your sister?

Multiple sclerosis. Two months before she and Al were supposed to get married, she found out.

He married her anyway? That took guts.

He didn't know. She was pregnant when they got married. He

didn't know that either.

Wow. Maybe that's what turned him into an asshole. What about your parents?

They knew, Margaret knew. The whole family knew but Al.

Those Dobermans of his are backyard monsters.

He makes money breeding them. Pays Margaret's doctor bills. Speaking of which, how much bread do we have, babe?

Eight maybe nine dollars.

I'll play till Hap and them get back.

Play till you get a thousand.

Damn straight.

They return in the Vista Cruiser, as Hap calls Al's station wagon. Still in his milkman uniform, Al's hosing the dog runs alongside the driveway. Even in white, he looks vaudeville-evil, the slicked hair, eyes deepset as traps, the sneering mouth. He has a flatboard butt and probably smells of wet dog and dog poop. He's coiling the green hose.

How was the zoo? Feel at home, Margaret?

Margaret flinches but holds her voice sweet. It was lovely, Al. WeeBee especially enjoyed the elephants, didn't you honey?

I saw this one, Daddy, he sucked a big peanut right up his nose!

That's great, pumpkin. Want to come help Daddy with the dogs?

Margaret, you and WeeBee can move into Mom and Dad's. They'd love it.

I've prayed so much, I have to believe God wants me here. I'm at peace with it, Ron.

Then you're the only one. Whenever I see the guy, he's meaner.

Oh gee, he's got his good side. He's awfully sweet to WeeBee. Oh stop talking about me. How's my talented, handsome brother?

Phoenix stands by the picture window in the family room,

watching Al with WeeBee in the back yard, leading one of the Doberman puppies on a chain leash, jerking it, supposedly instructing it. The animal backs up, flanks trembling. At one point, with WeeBee cross-legged in the grass, watching, Al boots its underbelly. The little girl's face lies flat as water. Al tows the dog, yelping, back to its cage, kicks its hip on the way in. The dog flattens, narrow head cringed between its front paws, flanks puffing.

Bastard, Phoenix says, her lips against cool glass. Idiot. Fool. Bastard.

At the dinner table, Phoenix asks if Tijuana's as gross as everybody says.

Who's everybody? asks Ron.

It's worse, Hap says.

Ever since I can remember, I've heard people talk about Tijuana. Hell pit, slime hole, den of vice and iniquity.

An erotic grin evilly lights Al's face. Some pretty hot action over the border ... my buddies and me used to drive over before me and Margaret was married ... there's places with what's called a donkey show and ...

Margaret interjects anxiously, Albert, please, WeeBee's ...

Oh, yeah, forgot. Nettled, he stabs around at his plate. Margaret, how many times do I gotta ask you to leave ham alone, stop puttin the fancy crap all over it. I like my meat plain, and any man worth a crap would say the same, right boys?

Wrong. Ron's voice is quiet, calm.

Well, we already know you're the exception ... a fruit liking fruit.

I think your glazed ham is delicious, Margaret. Phoenix double-loathes, triple-loathes this man. May I have more?

We oughta take Phoenix across the border after dinner, Hap says. So she can see for herself.

Oh you guys, would you? I've heard weird Tijuana stories for years. I just want to *see*—for myself. Like that song, "When You're Lost in the Rain."

That's Juarez, says Ron.

I know, but I love that song.

Ok, Hap stands up. Half hour, we're there. Let's split.

Let's help Margaret clean up first, says Ron.

Oh you kids are sweet, smiles Margaret. WeeBee starts pouting, demanding to go with, then demanding ice cream, the strawberry part of what she calls nepolodian. Phoenix decides that in a different home, and definitely with a different name, WeeBee might improve.

I'm telling you, if I had cancer and leprosy combined, I wouldn't stay a hot minute with that creep. What a jerk.

They're in the truck, passing a quart of beer.

Jeezlouise, what an asshole.

Margaret prays. She thinks she's doing God's will by staying.

Wow, that's so sad.

They've crossed the border, walking smack into a fiesta pink and purple Mexican sunset. Phoenix links arms with Hap and Ron, for protection. She giggles and gawks, rubbernecks, elbows Ron to give out more quarters to the children tagging beside them.

Stop it. Stop giving them money. Shit, it only encourages the little buggers. *Vamos.* Hap swats them off like fleas.

Every shop is open, shelves of garish pottery, faded piñatas strung along low ceilings, tables of watches, purses, radios, shoes, guitars, dresses, everything up for trade or sale. They turn down a street of dumpy, neon-lit bars, somebody outside each one hawking liquor and flesh. But it's Wednesday night and the street is blank. Phoenix marches them to a place where Fuzzyland drawls in pink neon over the curtained entrance.

Fuzzyland. *Fuzzy*land? Oh wow. Can I just see what's inside, pull-eeze you guys?

Are you serious? Hap looks almost disturbed.

Just for one minute. I promise. I need to learn about life.

They sit at a wobbly table shoved against a plywood platform, the only customers except for three college boys; like some shiny cockroach, the bartender scuttles behind the bar.

On the platform, a girl of maybe fifteen twirls in a white ankle-length dress, swaying to scratchy music, plucking her ruffled skirt, flirting it slightly above her bare knees. Phoenix decides she looks like a graduate of the same modeling course Phoenix's mother enrolled her in at J.C. Penney's one summer. Spin, glance over the shoulder, pause, smile, repeat.

Hap leans forward. Fuzziest thing in here so far is the sound system. The girl slaps off in stiletto heels to sickly applause from Hap, Ron, Phoenix, the college boys. Phoenix is feeling huge relief at the tameness of this place when a box speaker, swinging threateningly above the platform, buzzes, whines, starts blaring Spanish rock. A squat Venus of Willendorf, naked except for tiny slingback pumps, bulges hernia-like from behind a crooked cloth of black burlap. Squashy hands on hips, presenting all tremendous sides of herself, squatting until her knees crack, rolling on the dirty platform, her face revolving, a popeyed black Molly, cleaving her legs, thrusting her swollen dimpled flank right over Hap's warm glass of beer. Phoenix is stricken. Stricken. Should she smile to indicate she is no prude and can enjoy this uninhibited performance? Or should she display indignant compassion for exploited women by *not* looking at her, she feels this, too. Shouldn't she yank her aside, say what a dumb way to earn a living, go home, be with your baby. This girl has a baby. As she mashes her sallow, gourdlike breasts into the college boys' faces, milk silkily jets out each black, quarter-sized nipple. Shoving milk-loaded breasts in their faces—c'mon touch, wanna touch? Laughing at their moony baby faces humbled. She pumps one inky-nippled breast hard until milk hits one boy's lips, foams down his chin. Gets up, knees cracking and apart, the smile bitter, malicious.

Phoenix feels an odd stubborn paralysis, refusing to dishonor the primitive figure, its dry cunt clicking open and shut. She will be loyal to the figure on its hands and knees, ass pumping in bizarre insect-signal, tick-tock like the hula doll on the trucker's mirror. Hap slings an arm around Phoenix, dragging her ear toward his mouth. Check out the spot on the left cheek, on the ass ...

Phoenix nods.

Bullet hole.

She stares harder but then the woman swings a leg up, flips over, arching her pelvis toward the ceiling, up down in a fuck-simulate, head back, hair wagging. Phoenix uses up a minute or two trying to locate the bullet hole, its bluish-green scorch. Target practice by a drunken boyfriend, the baby's jealous father, the owner of the bar who brands his girls ... or what?

A man pushes through the street curtain, a wood tray with gum and cigarettes slung from his shoulders. He goes to the platform, she bends down so he can bury his head, hat and all, in the balloony crack of her breasts. In a while, his small wizened head pops out, beaming, and he flips her a stick of chewing gum. She pivots, flips the gum straight at Hap who flinches, lets it hit the table.

Phoenix passes her entire life beside this woman rolling in filth, swiveling her pointy tongue, opening and shaking in the faces of boys, taunting them in bad English to do it with her, do it. The college boys don't even look anymore, shaking their lowered heads, no.

Ron scrapes his chair back. C'mon, let's go.

Phoenix feels a goofy grateful thunking in her chest. Next to the curtained exit is a white man in a cowboy hat, three Mexican girls wrapped like foxskins around him, faces exotic with contempt; his face foolish, both hands thrusting deep into blouses. A staircase with red, lesioned carpet rises behind them.

The Fuzzyland sign flickers a flamingo pall over their faces.

Seen your minute's worth of sleaze? asks Ron.

Phoenix nods and Hap spits. This whole place stinks.

Not much is said on the short ride back to Margaret's. Rain hits and breaks over the windshield; Phoenix, having toked a joint with Hap, dozes, her head in Ron's lap, her legs flopped over Hap's. She stares into the green-lit dashboard, trying to see what the woman does by daylight, where she lives. The wipers flop and squeak over the glass.

Idle's rough, Hap says.

Yeah. I'm thinking about putting together one more lute, heading up to Big Sur awhile.

Ron says this, one hand off the steering wheel, drifting through Phoenix's Tijuana-smelling, tangled hair.

Sublimely clever! Being in love with a dead French poet. I keep a photograph of him inside my journal, torn from the *Illuminations*. Oh, he would have appreciated his effect upon me, how I am learning to surrender myself to the visionary, to disorder. Dismembering myself so as TO SEE. Dissecting the corpse still-vital, in order to glimpse its mystery.

There are kinds and kinds of Death. Levels, layers of Love. If I am to become an artist (oh, Poet of what?) I must take myself down to those most dark, coldest currents, the ones twisting, plunging steadily downward. Like that place with my family where we paid a dollar to go down winding stone steps in clammy, salty darkness, descending until we were underground and looking out to flat, brilliant, butted lines of sea and sky. At the bottom of the world, see how the sky splits open.

Who worships the goddess in the Tijuana whore? I should have liked to go home with her, see what things she did. Cooked. Ate. Washed. Talked. Dressed. Slept. Ordinary things. Nursed her baby. What does she dream of? Inspect her days and nights like a physician. Her corruption elevates us into mystery. Is the evil in her or in us who watch, is it a conspiracy of evils, or no evil at all, but some part of illusion, veil after veil lifting in gold and black, gold and black, revelation and secrecy?

For a few weeks, she lives at the Warehouse with Ron and Hap, employed by the Alpha Thrift Shop. Sorting ruined toys is dispiriting work, unloading bowed-in boxes of rubber dolls, animals with balding plush, games with missing parts, cracked toys, the overflowing boxes aligned like a train wreck. Phoenix sifts what's salvageable, which doll fixable, tagging a price on its tepid squishy heel. Sometimes a doll mews or bleats when it's picked up, but mostly they are inanimate, eerie, naked.

Phoenix got poison ivy from hiking to the Indian caves with Ron and Hap; its nasty red wine creeps from the tops of her sunburnt feet up her thighs. Her purple tights stick to the yellow ooze, her leg hairs pinch, glued in the sap; she steps off her clogs, skates her arch up and down her itchy calves. Standing on a cement floor eight hours a day, legs prickly and aching, flopping toys into reject bins, pinwheeling dolls and animals clunk or ploff in the bin, Phoenix feels sorry for children, sorry for toys, sorry for the world, an all-around hazy sorriness. She takes it out on the games, with broken mitsy pieces, dumping them with zeal. The salvaged toys get priced, Magic Marker on adhesive tape; she makes everything a quarter, the most neutral price she can think of.

Steering a grocery cart full of toys out the back room to the children's section, trying to arrange what she's saved to look cheerful; pert little toys on battleship gray metal shelves. Rocking the emptied cart past racks of men's, women's, children's, drapes, bedspreads, miscellaneous, the stuffed racks like dark-curled old shoe linings, musty with use. The first day, she'd snitched a velour shirt with leather lacings for Ron. Another day she'd taken a crepe dress with padded shoulders and rhinestone spigot buttons, and a tapestry of a medieval hunting party, a gold and green lute player in one corner. Her thievings lighten the colorless, mute hours, rejecting disengaged doll heads and limbs, the plastic and vinyl sediments of childhood.

Her second job, of shorter duration, is worse; hired with blatant misgivings by the highly strung manager of Clifford's

Hickory Chip House, Phoenix is issued a drip-dry blouse, a red bandanna, and a black taffeta circle skirt which she is supposed to hem to mid-thigh. She is to purchase her own nylons (hose, he calls them, twitching) and black boots (*not* ankle boots, he is agitated by the potential for error). She buys boots at the Alpha, a size and a half big, hems the skirt while she's panhandling with Hap so it winds up with a six-inch rise up the back of the left knee, a flaw she conceals by never turning her back on the manager. Work is a hyperactive trotting out of lukewarm hickory-chip burgers, cole slaw, and tater tots, tots being Mr. Clifford's maverick stand-in for french fries. "Remember or Pay: Six Tots To A Plate!" says a sign above the pick-up counter. The manager, known to all but himself as Hot To Tot, is a mess of fidgets: rocking heel to heel, wringing his hands like spotty laundry, popping his knuckles, recounting greasy tots, humming "Strangers in the Night." Phoenix snarfs butterscotch sundaes behind the partition, drops bottles of Coors down the crisp black depths of her taffeta pockets. Though she errs on the side of chattiness, customers ducking into laminated menus for refuge, she is never incompetent. The cook, not she, mixes up orders; she has never let go a pitcher of ice water down a customer's neck like the manager's favored waitress, whose bullet-nosed tits punch like fabulous weaponry through her starched white blouse.

The day Mr. Clifford personally, unexpectedly, appears in the philodendroned foyer, wreathed by cronies in nut-brown suits, his white hair a tendril of lard across the summit of his porkish skull, Texas emperor, moronic conqueror, he sways bulbous down aisles, eyes flicking, recording fault. The lunch waitresses peer over the partition to see whose station he will land in.

Oooh, Phoenix, yours.

No sweat. No biggy. Watch this.

She slunkers over to the booth in a penitential, pigeon-toed pose that pulls no wool over his narrowing gimlet eye. Why, he addresses his nut-brown suitmates, were they not issued a more attractive creature? The manager, doomed by his attachment to routine, by his mortal error in not sending the bullet-bosomed waitress, hovers, obsequious, miserable, behind slatternly Phoenix, performing little winkings and gnatlike motions.

May I ask what that *rag* is on your head?

Mr. Clifford, glaring at the Indian scarf knotted into her hair, squints past the first offense to the second, his blanching manager.

This ... creature has none of the qualities I require in my Hickory Chip girls. She is not attractive, she is not charming. I suggest you correct this situation. In the meantime, we would like to order lunch from *anyone* else.

Whoops. Phoenix is back behind the partition. I think I'm out of a job.

What happened?

Phoenix points to her scarf. This. Points to her lopsided hem. This. Not up to Barbie doll standards. Phoenix gulps down the last of her Coors, whips the bottle in the trash, just as the manager shows up blinking, an enraged rabbit, to fire her.

In a vacant lot next to the Warehouse, Ron and Hap sprawl in the gray limbs of an avocado tree, poaching. She has the grocery bag hoisted over her head; a clunk reverberates down her arms whenever an avocado gets pitched in. Bag loaded, they show up at the corner grocery where their five-dollar profit goes for beer and Hostess fruit pies, dotting the curb for lunch. Sluggish from noon beer and hot sun, Ron and Phoenix discuss going to Summerland, the local nude beach. Hap says nah, I hate that place. Still, they talk him into driving them, talk him into parking the truck, trudging down with them. Hap keeps saying forget it, man, I'm keeping my threads on.

Hap, says Phoenix, I've never done this either. His prudishness is oddly touching.

Yeah, well I'm not exactly into exposing myself in front of more than one person, preferably female, at a time. It's perverted.

Phoenix is half-antsy, wishing she could keep her clothes on too, let everyone else be naked, not her. But once they're on the beach, everybody stretched out naked, talking naked, playing naked frisbee, swimming naked, it seems weirder being dressed. Her clothes bump, scratch, confine, she has them off by the time they find a semi-private cove. Hap stays fully clothed in blue jeans, a long-sleeved shirt, and square black sunglasses, his face impassively facing the sea. Ron is in the water, his clothes humped next to Phoenix who's feeling hot buttery light pour over her, a grist of sand up the backs of her legs. The scabs from her poison ivy prick and sting. She's up on one elbow, sunk in dry womb-y warmth, when an ogler approaches, one of a spotty herd of furtive men in swim trunks and dark glasses who migrate past to stare at naked hippie girls. When she feels ogler's eyes feeding straight into her, Phoenix juts her hips, cleaves her legs so wide they cramp, a little idea she picked up in Tijuana.

Man, that dude, Hap keeps telling Ron, you shoulda seen him break into this fat panicky run. I mean she blew the guy away. Totally blew the pervert away.

The Warehouse, across from State Street beach, is a honeycomb of open lofts and studios for sculptors, painters, musicians. The first time she and Ron make love, Hap's out somewhere, and Phoenix has just witnessed a bizarre scene. Coming from outside, her eyes adjusting to the interior dimness, she hears this weird breathy gibberish coming from a gangly girl in white underpants, her breasts like tiny fruits, her face gaunt, yellow, black hair crazily chopped, face going all directions, eyes unnaturally wide. Mumbling, hiking over partly constructed walls, slipping in and out of scaffolding, monkey-agile, stealthy, as if in deep jungle. Blood dries in thin spills down her thighs; brighter blood keeps dribbling. The underpants a red hammock; red splatting the rough pine floor. Placing a finger in her blood, the eyes panicked but not just yet, the curl of lips indecipherable. Phoenix watches her eat blood, blood turning to sound out of a loosely parted, reddened mouth. Feeding on herself.

Ron, back to her, working at his bench, is physically perfect. His head a golden sphere, his back a muscled triangle, the split rectangle of his long legs. His hair hangs like straight platinum across his broad shoulders. But when he sits cross-legged on the mattress playing "Kemp's Jig" on the lute, a favorite, he says, of Queen Elizabeth's, and later, when they are in bed, all she can think of is the monkey-girl climbing all over everything, bleeding all over everything, eating a trail out of one world into another.

Phoenix's legs surprise him. Girls have smooth, shaven legs, but hers are springy with hair and caked with old pink calamine. They are in bed, sharing a bottle of wine, when Hap pounds up the stairs, stands in the doorway for a surprised half-beat before flopping himself across one end of the mattress. After a dumb joke about three of them together in bed, a remark revealing enough of Hap's loneliness and exclusion, he tries canceling it by punching Ron in the shoulder. Aw, you can't help it, guy, wrinkling his nose at Phoenix. Good thing there's nothin here to get too worked up about.

Ashamed, I give my body anyway, amazed anyone would desire its imperfection. The woman in Tijuana, grotesque, squatting, transcending that blunt, ugly, tough body. A goddess beyond beauty or horror or judgment, dancing with divine freakishness. The girl eating her own menstrual blood, what images of female are these?

The other day, Ron looked at me and said, wow, you're actually kind of pretty. And I felt what? Fool-grateful. I have a minor goal, not to love Ron's looks, a common predictable route, it's what he's used to and expects. No. I will love some other thing in him. The Artist.

Something in me demands to know ALL, but vanity, insecurity, a perpetual slippage between intention and act block my way. I've dropped most of this world's baggage, given the slip to the outside stuff, but what fiendish crap I carry within, more tenacious than the world.

Hap's insecurities surface through stiff jeans, white oxford shirt, hair cropped like mown dead grass, black sunglasses, his inner turmoil held in by this frozen uniform. He often dreams about being choked, wakes cradling his neck, stunned at being safe. He labors to act combative, cynical, asexual, remote, sleeps in the truck, leaving the mattress to them, takes off for days without saying anything, barges in grinning, saying the place reeks of sex.

When Ron hitches to Anaheim to sell another lute and meet customers from England, Phoenix feels suddenly wary, stuck alone with Hap.

The second Ron leaves, Hap appears in the shop. She is sitting on the bed, writing in her journal. Feigning writing.

He kicks the wall with the toe of his boot, not looking at her, thud, thud, thud.

Ron split?

Yeah, he did. He got a ride real early.

She goes back to writing, feigning writing.

Want to go for a ride or somethin?

A ride?

You know, a ride in the truck? Check out what's happening?

No, I don't think so, Hap.

He is by the workbench now, touching Ron's things, hefting and turning the tools in his hands, putting them back down.

Actually Hap, give me a minute? I've changed my mind.

He cruises the truck down a one-way street near the Warehouse, comes to a train crossing. There is no white safety rail, the red light is flashing. She hears him, let's see if we can make it, revving the engine, accelerating with a giant bounce onto the tracks. GodJesus. Out her window is a thunderous immensity of black, the train, rising over her.

The car coasts giddily into a curb. Hap's head and arms drop over the wheel. Her face feels ghostly, her body blown out like an egg.

Shit, she hears his muffled voice. Then lifting his head, he whoops, bangs on the steering wheel, yee! Goddamn, that was close.

You killed us. You almost fucking killed us!

He looks over, face ghastly, shiny, exultant. Sorry. Came pretty close I guess.

She jumps out of the truck, whams the door shut, starts running. She hears the truck backing up, lumbering after her. She swerves into an alley. The truck slavers, a big red cartoon dog, at her heels. At the end of the alley it pulls level with her.

Hey. Stop a minute.

Go to hell.

Hey. Don't be like that. I hate hard women. Stop. Hey, I'm sorry. That was dumb.

I'll say it was dumb, goddamn dumb. She's banging the heel of her clog on the plump red hood-snout. You nearly killed us both, and man, what a dumb stupid way to die!

His forehead on the steering wheel, Hap repeats quietly, I'm sorry, I really am sorry.

They've left the truck at the Warehouse, walked to the Sunday art show on the beach. Drinking beer, looking at paintings, jewelry, pottery, they keep going, end up in a bird refuge with tons of flamingos and black-legged birds with yellow banana-beaks diving in and out of a scummy, algaed pond. They hike up a long shady hill, arrive at the filigreed entrance to a cemetery with an unobstructed azure view of the sea. It is the hottest, most anchored part of the day; about a mile off, they see a speck, a toy mower racing between graves.

This oughta be a golf course, Hap says. The view is completely wasted.

They bend, squint, reading names and dates off the pale gray glare of stones, moving with careful politeness among the dead. Down a grassy slope, the percussive jet-jet-jet of a sprinkler hurls water across graves, wetting the stones. Phoenix feels mutinous in this fierce tidy place. Flips her clogs, sends them wheeling off the ends of her toes. One smacks a gravestone. She wants to pinch everybody awake. Hell with it. Hell with Hap. Unknots her purple top, flies it off her fingertips, sprinting, barefoot, bare-breasted, into a thick cypress wood overlooking the sea.

She strips off her jeans and squats in the greenish, chilly woods, letting urine glassily twist between her grimy heels.

A marble temple, pink and feminine, stands at the edge of the grove, a rumpled indigo band of sea behind it. Phoenix runs naked up the cool steps, peers inside to see the inscriptions. Two sisters in pink marble bunkbeds, one since 1938, 1952, the little sister's on top.

Hap's got her shoes, the violet top she'd thrown, holding her things watching her dance in the tinted woods like she's in some dream, some made-up stupid dream. Dancing around while he waits there, holding her shoes, her junk.

Stands so still between two tiny twisted trees. Ice from the marble wicks up her feet into her legs, branching through her chest, her fingertips pink and freezing. Hap is so still at the edge of the grove.

He shoves her against the rear wall of the temple. On either side of his closely cropped head is the sea, blue, white, rhythmically indifferent. His hands dig in her shoulders, his thumbs press the emptied pond of her neck.

You think bare ass and tits make you something special? Hey, you're nothing, man. You're another stupid chick, that's what. Ron's tight with me, he's with me.

Hey.

Hap unpins her, grins sheepishly. Just kidding, I wouldn't hurt you. Pinches one nipple. I'd get dressed if I were you. Before you get what you want.

What I want? God, Hap. I was *dancing*. Dancing. That's all I had in mind.

Right.

Right. What are you talking about? You scare me.

Damn straight. I'm a scary guy.

Journeybook

Hap has some dangerous thing brewing inwardly, imploding. His violence, repressed, and my pursuit of vision create humid, palpable tension. We cannot stand one another, we are too dangerously alike, wanting Ron, jealous of the other's claim. Ron, who has no conflict, no struggle. Safeguarded by simplicity, protected by beauty.

Ron, Hap and Phoenix are at a Mexican restaurant that used to be a house, bottles of Tecate, browning curls of lime piling up on the Formica table. Hap's lighting one cigarette after another. Phoenix won't look at him. Ron, oblivious, is talking about his trip to L.A.

So I'm at this party of lute pluckers, we have our professors of medieval sackbut, we have our ladies of the Renaissance in pointy hats, and weird food, man, dandelion wine, little pastry deals with minced meat or pork rinds and raisins and god knows whatshit, it's a reenactment of the old days. I'm there in my jeans, t-shirt, hair in a ponytail, the lutemaker. *Excusez moi,* the luthier. And these folks, these professors and other snobby types are kissy-licking me, I'm some sort of genius to them. I don't know, it was pretty weird.

You were a celebrity, Phoenix says.

Yeah, that's it, a celebrity. Some of the ladies came on to me pretty heavy, even a few men. This cellist from London, I kid you not, a three hundred and fifty pound, chain-smoking cellist, head of a cherub stuck like a cocktail cherry on top of this sliding land-fill of flesh, an amazing musician though, he breathed over me, kept wanting to know who I was going home with. Shit. I was nice, though, I said I had to go home to the wife, and that I was a Jehovah's Witness.

What did he say?

Nothing. Disappeared into the bathroom. Couldn't take rejection.

I know the feeling. Hap, dropping lit matches into his beer, looked meaningfully at Phoenix, who ignored him.

So, it was good business-wise. I got three orders, two lutes, one vihuela.

What's a veewaila?

Fancy lute. I don't know, actually, it was pretty nice. And what I'm starting to see is, if you let go, trust I guess, things work out.

Phoenix and Hap are silent.

Next morning, a note addressed to Ron sticks out from under the windshield wiper. Need to cut out. Go be an army grunt. Hah Hah. Time out to get my head straight. So. Take it easy, guy, but take it. Yours in sincerity, Hap.

Her last day at the Alpha Thrift Shop, Phoenix can't believe it. She can see Deal through the big amber window, pawing in a trash bin and fishing up, with theatrical gesture, a cigarette butt. He has that bashed-up hat on, pants cinched with rope, and a brown golf shirt. Does he know she works here, is this some improvised performance? She leaves the store to say something casual, winds up with him at a cafe with a pink Formica table, little gray boomerangs printed all over it, plus one of those miniature jukeboxes, staring over her Scotch-taped menu thinking he looks almost mad. Loony. He's been living in the theater building, in an empty room, alone. Still, she wants to even the score, her mouth full of club sandwich.

I'm involved with somebody.

Oh?

In love.

Oh?

Is that all you can say—a vowel?

Are you done? I'll pay.

Thanks, Deal. I'm busted.

She walks two blocks to see his room. Blank walls, water stains like orange vines, peeling ceiling, uncurtained windows, plaster silting the air. No furniture. Even with chalky film all over it, she recognizes his sleeping bag. Books strewn like trash over the wood floor, hundreds of books, and a purple tin ashtray spilling stubs and ash.

She bumps a toe on a stack of books. Reading all these?

Some.

He puts a bereft gaze to the crumbling ceiling. She will assume no guilt for his misery. In fact, she invokes cheerfulness.

Hey, Deal. You oughta get a ladder, do a real wild mural on the ceiling.

Too much up there already.

Well gee Eeyore, who's to say. Well, I gotta get back to the office, sort my toys.

No response.

I'm leaving town tomorrow. Funny I saw you today.

No response.

I'm going to Big Sur, there's this incredible commune my old man knows about.

Deal, in a gnarled upright fetal posture on his dusty sleeping bag, digs a garbage butt from his pocket, lights it. His psoriasis looks bad again. Spiraling smoke through the middle of a slat of sunlight, he looks Bolshevik, exiled.

How's your family?

He shudders.

I decided you can have the car.

I already sold it.

For how much?

A kilo and forty-five dollars.

Know what? Ron, sitting up in bed, his hair in gold rivers down his tanned shoulders, has the face and body, Phoenix thinks dreamily, of an angel. His fingers, tracing around her breasts, are now deep inside her, god I'm gone, Phoenix thinks, totally gone.

It's as if he knows, waiting until she is at that point, draws his fingers out.

You're too serious about sex. It's play, Phoenix. It's supposed to be a romp, you know. Fun. Don't take it so seriously. You know you have very pretty teeth.

Orthodonture.

Hm. Metal mouth like my sister. Want to fuck again?

Ron takes her not answering for yes. She tries to be like him, having fun.

Hap's first postcard says he's joined the army. The second and last says har har

Admit he's strange, Ron.

Nah, he's just pissed at me.

Would he do that, join the army?

No way. He'll keep out for no more ethical reason than to irk his old man.

The postcards, one a close-up of a flamingo's head, the other of a bunch of roadrunners, get tossed into the glove compartment.

Phoenix, pressed against Ron in the rattling, fuel-smelling truck, steadies a styrofoam cup of coffee between her knees. They're stopping for hitchhikers, the dusty faces bobbing like corks in her open window. Everybody crushes into the front seat, more in the camper, passing wine and weed. Later, when they have no one, Phoenix nuzzles her head in Ron's lap, the steering wheel thrumming lightly on her skull. All of a sudden, since they dropped this one couple off, she's started to slip, and Ron's asked twice what's wrong. She isn't able to say—pieces of herself sliding away one from another, contracting until she's nearly gone. Air slowed down, turning to stone, fills her mouth. She shrugs. Tired, I guess. Her voice shrunken, miniature. His arm clamps her shoulders, giving some blurred outline of Self. She's described this sensation to a psychologist, like a real slow leak in a tire, what I think of as Me leaking out of the body, I am air in this body and if something, I'm not sure what, punctures the skin of the body, I leak out, disappear. The psychologist had written everything down, all that Phoenix said, the busyness of his writing the only response.

They follow complicated directions from the stoned waitress at Nepenthe, twisting higher and deeper into national forest, grinding uphill on forest service roads, trespassing through green heavy silence and a pin-hot, almost fluid smell. Phoenix spots it first, the commune's purple and green banner flying limp from a tree limb. Ron bounces the truck off the road and they sit a minute. The engine ticks, heat and gas fumes shimmer above the red hood. They hear voices, a flute. Phoenix elbows Ron.
What if Hap came here to surprise us?
He hates communes.

Other than a few women wearing long skirts, everyone is basically naked. There is a wide ring of broad-hipped canvas tipis, a scattering of treehouses, a central cooking fire, bells, drums, chimes, banners like laundry flapping from trees. It has the look of a gypsy camp, gaudy and grimy. The faces that approach are sensuous, childlike, the names, Shadow, Wheat, Doreen, Cheyenne, StarCrow, surround, embrace her. Phoenix has tripped into a world of transparent creatures, fairies, elemental beings, children, playing in the forest, recreating the universe. There is freedom, blissfulness, the sweetish scorch of marijuana, a haze of dope, over everything.

Negative things happen right off. Ron starts sleeping with a girl named Rain, the same night Phoenix dances around the fire, dervish spinning, drums and flutes beating and piping like mad. This one guy keeps hassling her for sex, saying comicbook hippy stuff like he digs free-spirited chicks, etc. The best part of him is his chest—eight nipples, four ham-colored points down each side like a Hindu god, the one with twenty whirling arms and legs, eight semi-sacred nipples.

The commune eats soy and mung beans, cold kasha, oranges, and Chinese green tea. They pay a certain stoned amount of attention to daily readings of Tolkien, the Upanishads, Buckminster Fuller. Phoenix tries to meditate in the same detached, serene way they do but ends up watching Ron with Rain, spying on them, their matching blonde hair and tanned perfect limbs. Rain wears handmade leather sandals and a hip-skirt of feathers and shells. Her white teeth are big as tables, her eyes dimestore gems, her smiles dazzling and tiresome. Whenever she sees them together, which is every second, Phoenix chokes on coarse weedy thoughts, out of sync with Paradise and blaming herself.

She hikes off, wades upstream, finding forests similar to water with their fluctuations of temperature and light. Sleeps alone in Ron's sleeping bag, miserable, contaminated by what she thinks must be ego and selfishness. She needs to learn to lighten up, like Ron says, not be so serious. Let go.

Beautiful, Rain kept saying. Hah. Me beautiful? Tripping on STP, jumping off cliff after cliff, flopping up my own throat, the reason doped straight out of me.

Blown onto the greasy ceiling of the restaurant, pinned in an airless little triangle, looking down at myself here and there among the people, panic wounding my face, mouth this way and that, a clanging red shutter.

Me on the ceiling, grabbing Ron and her, throwing myself, hey, shit, ohmigod you guys, please, ohjesusshit, something's wrong.

On the redwood deck at Nepenthe, after dark, four of us tripping on clouds, constellations, and Vishnoo, my eight-nippled friend, fumbling a joint out of his pants, saying here's some heavy, mind-degenerating stuff. We smoke, go inside and Rain gets us dancing, me with Vishnoo but right away dropping like a rock down the black neck of something that keeps going, my face whistling into a long astounded O.

Scared as shit. Hysterical. Ron shushing, shush, everything's cool, no problem, you'll be ok. Everyone stoned to incoherence. Nobody makes sense. Vishnoo tries acting worried. Ron keeps repeating he doesn't know me that well. It falls on her to help. From the ceiling I see her polleny arms flatten the music, the noise, smoothing over the red Jello figures.

(I'll take her outside.) But I'm out—scooting around cars in the parking lot, gravel nicking my palms and knees. Wiped out, chuffing, I'm a ghost, god, I am a ghost. She lifts me to numbed, spectral feet so I can see, with good cunning, the highway, knowing I will march down its chalk spine letting cars pass through me like flame. But Rain is clever, locking her arms in a hard gate across my chest. I change tactics. Got to call the police. Get help. Police. She is gentle, no, no, you don't need that, we don't need that. (The hardest part, she says later, was persuading me not to call the police and get us all busted.)

Her rocking settles me so I can look around at things tremor-ing—trees, cars—rhythmic, shallow surgings of molecules. Trees are columns of intelligently heaving particles, upwardly roiling. Atoms shimmy, nothing is solid or still. Cars are not the dumb metal hunks I thought. My feet are whirrings of blue motion, my insides blurred with cells revolving in turbulent precision. I am a numb speck in some auric swirl.

Ron and Vishnoo find us in the parking lot, our backs against a trashcan, laughing. Howling, Rain keeps her gold arms buckled around me in the truck, keeps next to me when we get back to the commune.

Flat on my back, I exchange stars for body cells, chewing right along the sky, the black cavity of my body piles up, hot with stars. I walk inside a tree, pulled up its industrious watery veins, expire out its pliant, swelling tips. Rain sleeps beside me so I weasel up the hatched soles of her amber callused feet, slip under her bit-ten nails, between her table-sized teeth, roll up the rosily speckled cylinder of her throat, exit in fluorescent nimbus out her ivory skull.

By dawn, I've crashed, fallen from Vision yakking about my grandmother. Weak, I want my grandma.

They drive me, fed on kasha, vaguely lucid, down to the high-way. Dropping an amulet on a silver cord over my head, Rain gives me an address of friends in San Francisco. Ron hugs me, and we cry some. I say I might be in Mendocino in about a week. My sister is there. Carol. I have my tarot pack, cape, amulet, addresses, birth control pills, a baggy of Moroccan trading beads.

On the tarred shoulder of Scenic Highway One, my insides wobbly, my face inside out, if I can keep moving, sparking, hissing atoms like God, I'll probably be ok.

Dallas, this guy who picks Phoenix up, swaps his 12-string for her baggy of Moroccan beads while they're in Watsonville, an ash-yellow coastal town socked in with dull nubbed artichoke fields. Choke Capital of the World. They eat yogurt and sunflower seeds on the curb outside a health food store, discuss the downhill career of outdated Artichoke Queens.

It's late when they get to Santa Cruz, so Dallas says to crash at his place. She follows, rope-climbing a steep weedy incline to get to the cinderblock house. Inside, orange welts of material cling to the walls like rash, the floors Cheetos-colored shag. This total orange-osity wavers dangerously with multitudes of lit candles, is infested with musicians strumming monotonous electrified chords. Beaten by orange and amplified noise, Phoenix passes out on a mattress in an empty chilly room. In the morning, she navigates shag piled with snoring musicians, lunges over them toward the kitchen. She eats cheese, apples, stale cake, grabs a couple of beers, descends, hanging on the rope, to the road. That night she sleeps on the beach, cold under Deal's cape, her hair spongy with fog and salt, her head whirly from beer and no food.

The next day's ride is with a happy little tribe of goat farmers from Ukiah who offer to take her straight to San Francisco. She and Little Debbie the Dog share the bright windy truckbed. After a while, the truck goes up a dirt road into some cold, chard-green woods, stops in front of a funky homemade cabin. Inside are walls of black and white photographs, glossy blowups of elbows, breasts, hips, pubic hairs, ears, every little bodily thing. This, the photographer explains, is my wife. Elaine split two months ago, so I'm rearranging her into art. Phoenix thinks camera-chopping his ex-wife an obvious symptom of rage. Grimly, he cooks brown rice with chunks of yellow squash, passes out canning jars of red wine. The dog whimpers by the door, the kids glom onto "tiny tube," since there's no TV on their farm; Phoenix offers to take the dog out. Little Debbie, on her improvised bathrobe belt leash, hauls them both up a scruffy hill, cocking a leg even as they're still running. Phoenix flops on a discarded mattress,

81

twirly-sick from the wine. Little Debbie blunders against her, slops a corned beef tongue across her nose. Dogs have always liked her. Back inside, the kids are still slung on the couch, the air is thick with weed smoke, and it's been decided they'll crash overnight.

Phoenix wakes up to everybody spooning up oatmeal with rings of raw blue milk and gold lumps of peaches. They've set a place for her; when she comes in groggy from the outhouse, everybody acts radiant, like it's her birthday. Phoenix loves how nice people can be when they don't know you.

Hearing her pound a signal on the truck's rear window, they stop on Market Street to let her out. She imagines them herding goats, home-birthing rosy children in bright crocheted caps. She swings out of the truck, shoulders her pack, lopes up to the driver's window. They say she is welcome, anytime, to their farm, but are vague as to directions. The truck, a psychedelic goat's skull glued to its hood, day-glow streaking its faded sides, putts off. Little Debbie's tail whaps, the kids are skewed backwards, crunching silly faces at her, their little fingers waving peace signs.

She has to traipse in and out of five pawn shops before somebody gives her forty bucks for the 12-string.

Under the dressing room door, Phoenix sees the saleslady's feet pointed, suspiciously, straight at her. Stiletto pumps and cheap hose—aimed right at her, filthy hippy, sure-fire shoplifter, flower child/slut, rah, rah, rah … jeez. The minute she'd slunk through the revolving door in chewed-up bellbottoms, free box overcoat, bare feet, and floppy leather hat slammed on her bramble of hair, a phalanx of salesladies had set tight lip and gimlet eye on her. No one stepped forth politely, May I be of assistance, May I hold your hat and coat as you browse through our racks? No, they'd stalked her, stepped when she stepped, kept strict time. Now she's finally lugged an armload of fancy dresses into cubicle 4, kicking shut the door with her callused heel so the flimsy row of booths teeters on its brass hooves, and this one saleslady is stuck, feet aimed like weapons, three inches from Phoenix's.

She dumps the coat and hat in a corner, rolls off her smelly jeans, drops off her workshirt, same shit she's worn on the road for days. Her unwashed body looks fishy, hooked, sucked gray by fluorescence. Her eyes could double as deep-sunk screws. Adios, Phoenix, California road queen; Hello, Mary Lou, long lost, impoverished grandchild. She seesaws a red mini-dress over her head, does the J.C. Penney spin, hands on poked-out hips. The red dress pushes her face into focus. Next we have Miss Mary Lou in a fashionable yellow paisley with black shoulder buttons like cootie heads. Oh, but the bummer is her *face*. She widens her eyes, squinches her eyes, stacks her hair, lets it drop. Tries a slew of angles, sticking out her tongue at the pasty skin, nasty bone, smarmy eye, queer mouth, stink-o nose. Hell with it. She forgets the other dresses, stuns the phalanx by putting down cash for the red dress along with two sets of white fishnet pantyhose. The dress gets folded into a shopping bag, the yellow paisley's stashed under her hat.

Down the block, in a Walgreen's ladies' room, Phoenix shakes the paisley out of the greasy bin of her hat, climbs into the red dress, tugs her boots out of her pack, steps up to a sink loaded with wadded brown towels to wash her face with a squish of pink from the metal box, scrubs at her front pieces of hair, rinsing them under the tap, turns a hot blower on her face. Galumping in too-big boots down an aisle of the store, she palms a white lipstick, drops it in the shopping bag. Her road clothes, from the free box in Watsonville, get left on the pink, leaking floor of Ladies.

Heading to a bus stop, Phoenix comes up to a crowd clamped around two drunks cuffing and mostly missing one another, one bubbling blood out of his smooshed nose like a trick he's learned. Passive crowd, wow, here's TV.

What's the deal? she asks around.

That guy in the black shirt says the other one took his money. Five dollars.

She pushes right up, lays two five dollar bills on the sidewalk between them. Smooshed-Nose squeezes up a bill between his fingers, churchlike. Black Shirt, leering, pockets her money.

Gee thanks, sis. Whoah, you got bedroom eyes, anybody tell you? Real bedroom eyes.

You wouldn't be pulling my leg, would you?

I'd like an opportunity.

The crowd dirtylaughs a little.

Jeez. Buy yourself some food.

After the bus, Phoenix walks six or so blocks to her grandmother's. This near the bay, with its tobacco-black, rotting wharves, with the sun near setting, the air drenched in medieval gold, the sky shimming like milky grout between immense gray and rose sides of apartments, slipping in disciplined combings between precise forms, people move around the bases of these immaculate, climbing geometries, distracted, insignificant.

A ball-bellied black doorman, bursting out of green and gold livery, swings wide the glass door, so theatric and overly cheerful it embarrasses her. In the mirrored elevator, a circle glows around 14, a nightlight. She drubs the white thumb of lipstick around her lips, hefts her pack, steps out of the elevator into a lush carpeted hall with an odor of fried meat. Passes evenly spaced doors like a dream line of flat white cards, finally pressing an ivory button with the correct number. She hears muted shuffling before the brass spy cover slips open, and a gray eye takes up the roundness.

My gracious, dearie. It's our Mary Lou. Mary Lou's here. She's out in the hall, for heaven's sakes.

Phoenix hasn't heard that name, her old name, in weeks. The brass chain drops, her grandmother opens the door.

Oh please—fastening on her grandmother like good, firm land, like the one place she's found safe in weeks—let it be what it was. Climbing past her parents and unremarkable childhood, going back in perfect Time. Gramma's Mary Lou.

* * *

Her grandmother's furnishings are arranged exactly as they had been in the old house. Twin mahogany tables, green velveteen couch, Manet and Utrillo reproductions in baroque frames, pigskin chests, carved ivory screens from China. She considers everything her grandmother's, but her grandfather lives here, taking sterner, darker steps to his wife's liltings and perchings, treading with the somber weight of park statuary.

Always, her grandmother has worn a beige or navy sheath with a Peter Pan collar and skinny belt, silk stockings with rubber and metal garters. Her black heels, from Italy, cost over one hundred dollars. This muted diminutive form is balm and honey, from it proceeds a perpetual subdued flow and bliss of wealth. Phoenix remembers never having enough of what could be purchased, the privacy of expensive things, the holy counterfeit hush issuing from rare objects, exorbitant spaces. And Phoenix remembers this woman, this grandmother, in her navy or beige sheath with its hard skinny belt and stiff sleeves, the pernicious blood sallowing her skin, the slushy blue hair and indulgent dipped-in face, nourishing, no, bloating her!

Children never regret being spoilt. How could she resist being allowed to eat or not eat, do nothing or everything, breathe whenever or however she chose? Two weeks each August, as Mary Lou, she slept on starched, ironed sheets, woke at dawn to the hollow roar of zoo lions down the street. For breakfast, she was given coffee cut with milk in a doll-sized, pink and gold cup. She and her grandmother watched morning TV, "The Price Is Right," comparing closest guesses. When her grandmother took a rest after lunch, Mary Lou watched "Queen for a Day," hooked on the potent dreadfulness of grown-up lives. Domestic anguish separated and stacked like poker chips, every contestant's teary eye on the applause-o-meter ... what happened to the women uncrowned by their tragedies, the ones going back to lives nasty enough to have earned them a spot on the show? These were upside-down fairy tales Mary Lou never missed.

Her grandfather, before his retirement, ate his eggs peppered and sunnyside up, read the *Sacramento Bee,* drove to work in a celery-colored Cadillac. After retirement, he ate the eggs and read the paper, but then, in Bermuda shorts and plain white t-shirt, weeded his kidney-shaped dichondra bed. When her grandparents turned in, as they called it, after lunch, Mary Lou got to watch more TV, drink gingerale floats, shivering and indolent, in the green-and-white air-conditioned house.

Her grandmother never learned to drive; a taxi took the two of them downtown to expensive stores, to the same dark restaurant with gold-corded menus, rigid tablecloths, pale curlings of butter, and brittle rolls with airy centers. Mary Lou learned to heft silvery cool knives, cut into flushed slabs of prime rib, press down with etched fork, wrecking the French pastries. Returning home, they counted on grandfather's whistlings and "whoo-whoo"ings as they modeled the fancy contents of their shopping bags. This train-sound, emanating from the blue cigarette haze that was killing him even as he sat in his leather chair, satisfied them by its ritual and variation; the more a thing cost, the more steam he blew. His immense white back was strewn thick as a lily pond with velvety splots of moles. His second best feature was a library Mary Lou was free to muck through. He had been a surgeon, so a number of shelves were taken up by fat leatherbound medical texts. She tugged down the fattest first, its maroon edge whoofing into her belly, grew intimate with color plates of tropical afflictions, turning straight to distended and scabrous penises, uncircumcised, with melon-sized scrotums. Perplexed-looking men, each with a penis ballooned, drooping past his knees. Elephantiasis, the small print diagnosis. Mary Lou took occult pleasure, from the first thudding of the book against her belly to later imagining, within the colorful hyperbole of disease, what the dimension of normal, unafflicted men might be.

By the end of August, after this orgiastic submersion in television, perpetual sweets, and exotic male trauma, Mary Lou stepped from the plane, straining chubbily within one of too many new party dresses (a particular exasperation to her mother: why can't she just give you money so we can buy what you need, gym shoes, for one thing). Pale and secretive from her association with male anatomy, glutted on cookies and sleep, Mary Lou was, at best, unresponsive. Her mother, handed back this doltish, monosyllabic daughter, this prepubescent lummox, realized how dearly she had purchased two weeks' freedom.

Did you at least swim? she asked.

Her grandparents' neighbors had a pool, but since her grandmother couldn't swim, she was, illogically, afraid Mary Lou might drown. Mary Lou agreed to swim once, with her grandmother sitting in a chair by the side, so she could answer her mother truthfully.

While Mary Lou was this mystery of malleable youth-stuff, keeping her family in hopes of some possible still-dormant distinction, her grandmother regularly announced to dinner company that, in all likelihood, her youngest granddaughter would marry Prince Charles. Their birth dates were the same, and could anyone overlook the uncanny resemblance to Princess Margaret? This logic stunned and enslaved Mary Lou, who looked forward to easy wealth, a royal and doting husband. These over-reachings for grandeur and class, irresistible since they involved her, set Mary Lou's mother on an opposite course of insane headaches, compelling her at times to peck at her spoilt daughter through the blankets with the heel of her cheap shoe. Having to live and breathe in a place of such disappointing proportions, her marriage; in suppressed fury over her own blown expectations, why should she remain calm, watching Mary Lou plumped and petted into a spoilt, naive princess, and by her husband's mother? Who else could she blame?

In those Augusts of Mary Lou's youth, blissful damage between the three women was wrought.

Now Phoenix wants to shake her grandmother like a toy bank, shake out of her things the way they were, plunder her childhood. Instead, she lies on the familiar starched, ironed sheets, listening to her grandfather cough-wheeze-cough for wrenching blue minutes, her grandmother's voice in anxious, frail counterpoint.

Phoenix gets her own coffee, climbs a chair to search cabinets for her pink and gold cup. God, how do they manage? She winds up fixing eggs and toast while her grandmother dodders about, wondering what meal this is, which day this is, who's she, the maid? No, Phoenix repeats doggedly, I'm Mary Lou. Mary Lou. Your granddaughter.

Phoenix dials for a taxi while her grandfather chuffs and gasps over to his leather chair, the oxygen tank behind it, a khaki green bullet.

Phoenix has chosen I. Magnin's; the shoe salesman is curt with her grandmother, dismissive of her. In Ladies' Dresses, a saleswoman with a slipshod French accent is unctuous, bored. Phoenix's mother claims her grandmother buys clothes and never wears them; the sheaths, cashmere coats, shoeboxes pile up and glut her closet, price tags still attached. Her grandmother insists Phoenix buy something, pick something, so they take the perfumed elevator up to Juniors with its strobe lights and Rolling

Stones tape. Phoenix shoves around racks of leather, velvet, and paisley while her grandmother, knees fastidiously crossed, perches on a blue neon wave. Phoenix chooses an embroidered suede coat with a fleece lining.

Her grandmother moves haltingly, as if her Italian shoes don't feel the sidewalk, as if they aren't connected to any ground. Phoenix steers her by the elbow to the sides of buildings, out of people's way, helps her up shallow steps of the hotel and into the engulfing lobby with its diamondish sprays of chandeliers, oriental carpeting, arterial blue leather couches. Phoenix tells the maitre'd her grandmother's name; they sit to wait on one of the leather benches. The gray mink stole (wrap, her grandmother calls it) keeps slipping off her hunched shoulders, her purse gapes, stuffed with loose bills, linting Kleenexes with scarlet cabbage kisses—a toy purse. Her silk stockings sag, her knees and thighs part, weak bannisters leading to an open darkness, similar to the purse.

When her name is called, they perk up. They remember how to do this, order the prime rib and Yorkshire pudding. But her grandmother doesn't touch hers; she rarely eats anymore, and Phoenix can't eat because she is newly conscious of her knife coolly plying into a bloody plank of flesh. The plates, untouched, are removed. They demand French pastries from the domed cart. Her grandmother gouges at the iced napoleon with oblivious greed, orders a second, eats that, while Phoenix aches over this hobbled outing, and, worse, entertains Dostoyevskian ideas of stealing money from her grandmother's purse while she is busy talking about friends dead and dying. For a minute, Phoenix falls evilly silent over their coffees and third helpings, this time pastry swans and eclairs.

Grandmother? Thank you for the coat. I love it.

The coat, Mary Lou? I hope it's the right thing. Is it the right thing, this time of year?

Perfect, really. Thank you so much. Grandfather doesn't look very well.

We don't go out anymore, he has to be near his oxygen. Huffs and puffs so without it. Every morning, he takes the elevator to the garage to start the car, let it run. Just sits down there in the car. He loves driving, poor man.

Women at surrounding tables clack mouths and dishes, shopping bags mulched around their feet, while Phoenix and her grandmother sit, ghosts, scarcely visible to one another. Phoenix doubts they are there except a waiter keeps bringing and removing things, and a water boy relentlessly splashes water. Her grandmother, forever a willing slave to fashion, has not said a word about her mini-dress, black boots, white lipstick. She doesn't see her, not as she is, maybe she sees nine-year-old Mary Lou with the Buster Brown haircut and freckles, in the lace-collared, velvet party dress. Prim and mute.

Phoenix navigates them to the marbled, heavily scented bathroom with its uniformed attendant, watches her grandmother scrabble out from her purse a twenty-dollar bill, which the attendant impassively, dishonestly, accepts. She guides her back down the carpeted steps with slick brass railings. The doorman opens the taxi door. Oh, god, Phoenix is realizing. She did this for me. She has no vanity left for shopping, no appetite for hotel lunches. She did this for me.

After her grandparents turn in, Phoenix dials the number a friend in Big Sur had given her. A sullen female voice picks up.

Yeah?

Uh, my name's Phoenix, and a friend gave me your number, she said maybe I could crash at your place if I needed to.

Who's that?

Rain. We met up in Big Sur.

Oh sure, far-out chick. Well, no biggy. Where are you now?

My grandparents' place, but I can't stay.

People drift in and out, it's definitely crazy, but if you like craziness, no problem.

Good. She has a place to go. She cleans the kitchen, makes two cheese sandwiches, wraps them and puts them on plates, sets a can of vegetable soup on the counter. Takes a hit off her grandfather's vodka, sponges off the dining room table. His ashes are all over the placemat and some egg yolk, so she washes and dries it. Her grandmother's place is spotless. Phoenix runs his glasses under water, polishes them. Otherwise the apartment's tidy. There's practically nothing to do. Finds a tube of glue and pieces together a broken cereal bowl. Opens the refrigerator, pulls out moldy fruit, turned milk, a flabby heel of lettuce. Patching and getting rid of chaos, infirmity, evidence of mental collapse. She stacks newspapers, lines up empty Coke bottles, goes into the library, folds her bed back into the couch.

She hears them in the bedroom, awake. They will be sitting on the worn edges of their beds, her grandfather in white undershorts and white t-shirt, her grandmother in one of her lacy beige slips. Oh dearie this and dearie that, real conversation. She's never known what they say to one another every afternoon and so earnestly. They'll talk up to an hour. There will be her grandfather's mahogany dresser with the linen topcloth, the silver and copper handful of change by the photographs of her sister, Carol, and herself when they were nine and fourteen, in black velvet dresses. There will be her grandmother's beige-skirted dressing table with the silver-handled comb and brush set, bobby pins, buttons, foil wrapped Sucrets in the green ivy dish. What they say is private, mysterious, but at least she knows how everything looks.

She stands in the hall, close to their sweet, familiar, failing voices, wanting to save and retrieve them, wanting as if it could be done. Grandmother and grandfather. Childhood.

She wipes the bathroom sink for them, rinses the cup.

Watching "M*A*S*H," he mixes his five o'clock martini. During a commercial, Phoenix puts on her new coat, but halfway into his ritual "whoo whoo's," her grandfather turns to suck oxygen from the green tank rising like an implacable landscape behind his leather chair. His face, purplish, stubbled, tries again. Whoo whoo. She hates this obstinate courage, the need for it.

When her grandmother comes out of the bedroom in her silk navy sheath and real pearls, Phoenix mentions the soup and sandwiches for dinner, that she's going across the city to stay with friends; that she'll be taking a bus up to Mendocino to visit Carol. Specifically talks about a bus, about Mary Lou riding a bus, nothing about Phoenix hitchhiking her way up the coast.

They walk with her into the neat narrow foyer, her grandmother pressing money into her hand, something she always does, something Phoenix, guiltily, counts on her to do. Kisses, embraces. Her grandmother tugs out the hanky she keeps stuffed in her sleeve, mops at her eyes.

You're the light of our lives, you know, dear, don't you?

The same man holds the door, his coat winging in the salt wind off the bay. She looks him halfway in the eye, says thanks.

On a city bus, wearing her coat, Phoenix irons the wrinkled hundred dollar bill with her palm. It smells of lilac. Dumb money, money she knew she would get, making her cry.

The bus hisses down rain-inked streets, its ashen interior unsparing of faces broken from work, each with a clayey stillness. Phoenix stares through rivulets limned with bus light, tailing down the window. When she pulls the buzzer line, the bus heels, squarely obedient, to the curb.

Going into a corner grocery that smells of vegetables rotting in damp earth even though its narrow wood aisles are stacked only with canned goods, she buys chicory blue daisies, ginseng tea, Chinese sesame biscuits. Someone in a purple and orange dashiki and striped bellbottoms, his hair a raisin frizzle, stands behind her as a balding man in a grocer's apron counts change into her hand, dandles her fingers, fondling her upturned hand flopped childish and pink on the wood counter, squeezing her fingers one by one, his crabbed face shrewd on the nickels and dimes, his hands disassociated and hot, greedy, wicked as any lover's. She's too thrown to ask him directions, waits outside for the guy in the dashiki to come out. Obligingly, he points up two steep blocks she must climb to the Shrader house. He also points down.

City's idea of an obstacle course, all the dog turds. Matter of agility. Hey. The old dude in there is crazy but harmless.

Navigating around rain-slushed shit, Phoenix passes a head shop, a used bookstore, a Korean restaurant, a dry cleaner's and a herpetarium before reaching a second, steeper block of three-story apartments with flat, watered, granite faces.

Light blurs through the pink, black, and orange stripes of an Indian cloth sagging down a glass and oak front door. She presses the bell until someone with hair in brittle black tufts, a black leather jacket, black pants, and boots unlatches and opens the heavy door.

You the chick that called? Wow, is that rain out there? I'm Cherish.

Sitar dronings vibrate down a meatloaf-smelling hallway. Cherish lopes backwards, facing her, skinny arms and legs churning like a spider's.

We sorta finished dinner. Might be something left.

That's ok. I ate. Thanks.

Six or seven women are sitting around a square oak table. The kitchen walls are glazed citrine; ferns, spider plants, coleus, toothpicked avocados sprawl green, dripping all over. Phoenix leans into the doorframe, awkward; talk lags to nothing as they stare at her. She pushes her arms, with gifts, toward the room.

I brought some things to, um, thank you for letting me stay here.

The women continue to stare so bluntly, blood hits up into her face.

She just got here from Big Sur. You guys remember that chick, Rain? Sorry, I forgot, totally spaced your name.

Phoenix.

God, great name. *Fab*ulous!

The woman saying this breaks from the others, pushes over. Like Margaret Mead, Phoenix thinks, owlish and squat, bobbed brown hair, square glasses, boxy chin, a gargly voice. She thrusts out a hand, pumps Phoenix's with almost senseless energy.

I'm Luci. Want some wine? God—daisies—fabulous, eeeh, what's this—ginseng—farout—oriental aphrodisiac—and Cherish, look—you die for these cookies.

Eyes cropped in black, lips necro-white, Cherish angles over so Margaret Mead can slip an arm around her spidery black middle.

Mmm, nummy biscuit … Luci wedges a cookie against the chalky lips which part stingily to bite.

Gulping a few glasses of wine, Phoenix attains both a modest buzz and an artificial confidence. She's dead-smack in a nest, clan, commune, swarm, festal gathering of lesbians. Rain neglected mentioning this, or maybe figured Phoenix was a latent and sent her on purpose. Paranoid. Ridiculous. So what, she has nothing against lesbians, she's just never *known* any—she should drop it into the conversation, casually, that she is straight. Right away.

94

She visits the bathroom down the hall, with its floor-to-ceiling collage of mostly nude women. The light fixture's got a fat red bulb so she and the toilet, sink, tub, and the women in the collage all flare like accidents.

When she comes back to the sulphurous, jungly kitchen, the women, except Cherish and Luci, have all split. Apparently sulking, Cherish is viciously pinching leaves off plants while Luci scoots around collecting and crashing dishes into the sink.

Do all those women live here?

No. They're Althea's friends. She works at the herpetarium and does a nightclub act with snakes. Cherish and I have been here longest, almost six months. Althea is never here or else here with somebody she's picked up. If you decide to stay more than a week, we can figure out rent money, chore-sharing, that kind of stuff.

I don't think I'll be here too long.

Cherish takes her black racy eyes to slits. We freak you out?

No. God, no.

Cherish smirks, scuffs her black boot. You oughta see your face. Straight, right?

Phoenix nods, her face feeling hot.

Hey, we won't hassle you. I'll be on my best behavior though I can't speak for Luci the Luster.

Luci shoots out of the kitchen just as Cherish winks at Phoenix. Come on, I'll show you Althea's room, where you'll stay. Then I gotta study.

Luci's in premed. She wants to be a pediatrician.

Yeah. Cheri *was* in premed. She dropped out to be my housewife or something.

That's where we met.

Slicing with dainty intent into male froggies.

We found very little.

To our liking.

Except each other.

95

Luci flips the light on as Cherish says with deadpan timing, Althea's into snakes.

The room smells damp, medicinally bitter. Glass cages line the walls. A mattress in the middle of the floor has a pink-and-black striped bedspread tugged neatly over viscerated insides. The room, otherwise, is empty.

Althea's gone a couple of days. You can stay here if snakes don't freak you out.

Phoenix points to a glass cage swarming lumpily with white mice. What are those?

Snakevittles.

Ohjeez.

Althea's our undependable, exotic household member. She's also maddeningly bisexual.

Who cares, I *love* that roto-rooter hair. Cherish twirls her fingers out from her head …

Sure you don't mind about the snakes? Luci sounds absurdly maternal, even her blouse sleeves, chunky and white, cut above the elbow, look overly competent, practical.

I guess if they stay in their cages and I stay in mine, we'll be ok.

They're always conked out anyway, Cherish says with flippant distaste.

With twin eerie smiles, Luci and Cherish leave her in a room filled with snakes, a cage of wavy mice. She flops, face-up, stoned, on the mattress.

A Medea-haired figure in a red satin cape fills the doorway. Phoenix sits up, blinking in overhead glare.

So-o-o, said Wee Bear, who's that sleeping in *my* bed? The figure clomps across the room in green army boots without waiting for an answer, kneels by one of the cages, gets up, knees cracking, There baby, crooning, did you miss Thea, baby? Thea missed you. Turns, facing Phoenix with a sly smile, the snake coiling like black tubing around her skinny, pale arm. Nobody told me I had a visitor.

Sorry to be in your bed.

No, such a treat, no, baby? She nuzzles the snake, scraping in her ugly boots closer to the bed. Phoenix has been sleeping in her jeans and work shirt.

I'm Althea. Her hand is dry, sparky feeling.

Phoenix starts to sit up. Hey, I can cut out, find another …

Absolutely no, never. Stay. There's a sofa bed in the living room, I have a friend with me anyway, he's using the shower. And we're both starved so we'll be feasting and foraging in the kitchen. I'll bring Zuni (Phoenix assumes this is the snake) back later … but I won't turn the light on. Althea clumps into the hall, the snake vining, syruping, up her neck. Suddenly her head, as well as the snake's, cranes back in the doorway.

I could use somebody at the herpetarium tomorrow. Easy stuff, feeding, cleaning cages. Can you use an extra twenty bucks or so?

Sure.

I'll wake you up. Or you wake me. Whoever's first.

To keep up, Phoenix literally has to trot beside Althea down poop-strewn, foggy streets to the herpetarium. When they stop in the corner grocery for doughnuts and coffee, Phoenix notices the dirty old grocer isn't there. Althea, over six feet tall, in her ruby satin cape, her spiraling brambly red hair with its aureole of pinkish frizz, talks with vibrant, thunderous energy that draws planetary attention.

Phoenix feels extinguished and mousy, holding the bag of doughnuts and two coffees while Althea flails around in her paisley carpetbag for keys. The herpetarium's exterior has two plate glass windows swirled with white paint so you can't see in. Between the windows is a plain wooden door with a barely legible note, Herpetarium Hours: erratic.

Awright, hail mary, here's the little sucker. Her spindly white fingers jiggle the key, push up with the key, down on the door, prise with the toe of one boot until the door grudgingly cracks from its swollen jamb.

She flicks a light switch, sails toward the back, leaving Phoenix in a supermarket-sized room, its low ceilings lit by skinny veins of white fluorescence. The air is muddy, humid, stifling, the exact smell of Althea's room but concentrated. Row after row of metal tanks on wooden stands, and along the walls, stacked rows of glass terrariums. The floor is marbled light and dark green linoleum, the place looks and smells greenish yellow. Fetid.

C'mon in the back, I'll get you started, Althea is hollering. Phoenix tiptoes up to the tin cradle nearest her, looks in. A golf bag-sized alligator, sunk in water, beveled snout resting on a flat rock, one eye locked, protuberant, on her, the other shut.

Hi there. (Asleep? About to lunge?)

She walks down weirdly silent rows of reptile life, alligators, snakes, turtles, lizards—silent herself, unnerved.

Althea, perched on a Formica countertop by a deep cement sink, legs crossed yet frenziedly swinging, chomps a doughnut with extra-wide jaw swivels, gestures to a table with the doughnut bag on it.

Hurry, eat, coffee's cold as a witch's tit. This place is so sca-rewed. Charlie's got hepatitis, Leo's quit, the guy that owns the place is down in Mexico chasing snakes.…I'm supposed to han-dle the whole frickin' circus till he gets back if he gets back. He's been bitten twice on these expeditions. Jeez. The cages need cleaning, a shipment of frogs are gonna be here any second, we're short feeder mice, it's another fine dill pickle we're in, Ollie, Althea rolls her eyes at Phoenix. But hey, no biggy … you're here to save me.

Phoenix's smile is wan. What do I do?

Everything, dearie. Everything short of blowing up the place.

Phoenix passes two squeamish hours unpacking a crate of Manitoba leopard frogs, unleashing them in aquarium tanks padded with damp sphagnum, figuring how to grip their clammy twitching hind legs. Takes hamburger packets out of one of sev-eral beat-up refrigerators, goes around pelting raw meatballs at the turtles. She carries and cleans cages, drops mice by boudoir pink tails into the evil snake tanks. Althea does some kind of desk work, keeps a radio blasting, singing along, way off-key. A pair of ferrets, loose, streak flat and brown under tanks and down aisles. The huge area, fluorescent, hot as a desert, moist as a gym shower room, makes Phoenix queasy.

You could wear a bathing suit in here, she announces, going past Althea with a platter of raw meatballs.

I have, but the guys got excited, know what I mean?

At first Phoenix refuses to pick up the snakes, she squeals uncontrollably and backs up. Althea lets them ripple and slip over her, two, three at a time, her face accepting their needle-thin flickery tongues.

Hold this one, he's a California boa, they're real gentle. Just stay très, très calm, pretend you're his hot sunny rock.

The snake feels cool, dry, muscular; she is appalled by his grip on her arm, sliding up toward her face, tongue wickering, tast-ing, sensing her. Slithering under her arm, around her neck and shoulders, winding down around her waist. She whispers, panicked, get him off me. Althea laughs, the snake pouring off her arm in a long S, plops back in his tank.

Phoenix is in the shower, scrubbing with a loofah, feeling pasted with reptile slime, turtle goo ... keeps tipping her head, letting water roll down her throat and gargling—argh, argh—she's on an argh when Althea bangs into the steamy room. Phoenix can see the misty carrot top of her hair above the shower rod.

You got Zuni with you?

I hope not.

He's not in his cage and he's not anywhere in my room.

So when Phoenix comes out of the bathroom, she is enlisted in a full-scale hunt.

Luci, on hands and knees, peering under the living room couch, says, symbolic all this, you realize: Daughters of Sappho search fruitlessly for the long black snake.

Cherish, hands cupped around her mouth, yodels down the hall. Here, snakee snakee snakeee ...

Godsakes, it's not a pig, Althea snaps.

So sorry. How do you suggest calling a snake?

This is worse than a gerbil, Luci says, hauling up sofa cushions.

You don't call snakes. They aren't servile. They're not dogs. You have to move very softly, intuit, look in dark, warm places. Althea sounds passionate.

The basement, Phoenix says. Anyone checked the basement?

You, Nancy Drew. I'm getting us all wine and a joint or two, this could be an extended search and rescue. Luci heads for the kitchen.

Leaning on a window sill, Cherish draws a snake in the dusty glass. Maybe if you dangled a pretty female snake out in the open? Or a tasty fat rat?

God. Forget it, Cherish.

Phoenix still hasn't gone down to the basement, she's looking for flashlight batteries in kitchen drawers, finding everything but.

Althea, in a skimpy black mini-dress and boots, directs, they stop to take hits from the wine bottle and off a weak joint. Cherish puts on Sergeant Pepper but Althea says no, this is a search party first, a party party after.

Why can't we do both together? Cherish whines. This is a terrible thing to have to look for, a contact lens is better, it can't move, I mean it stays within a certain perimeter, radius, whatever. She wanders vaguely out of the living room. Later, they find her prone, face down on the carpet in the hall.

What are you doing?

Shh. Hush you muskies.

Althea is fastest. Intuiting the snake, feeling what it would feel, right?

Cherish nods.

She jiggles Cherish's rump with her boot heel. You may be back in my life again.

Cherish sits up, slaps her knees. Got it! He's headed back to Alabama, that's where he's from, right? He's homesick.

Down in the basement with a dinky flashlight, Phoenix is losing hope, heart, etc. She pats her hand along exposed moist pipes, the flashlight giving off a watery beam. Half the basement is an unused apartment with a bed, an old desk, dozens of cases of Perrier, and French breadsticks. There's even a tiny kitchen with huge pipes overhead. She runs the light around the tangle of pipes, stopping at one above the stove. Zuni hangs from it like an acrobat, glaring at her. Suddenly, he drops to the white enamel stove and coils. Should she clamp something over him, a pot lid, box, or something? No, better run upstairs.

At the top of the basement stairs, she meets Luci.

Coming down to help, she cackles, then Phoenix feels a mouth on hers, a warm gluey kiss that shocks her, sending a familiar electrical zigging down her spine. Her silly mind, she overhears it, wow, like a male mouth, same kiss exactly.

She unsticks from Luci's mouth. Ah. Found him. Down there. Zuni?

On that little stove.

How do you know he's still there?

I don't.

By the nacreous gloom of the flashlight, Althea fondles her snake, making his forked black tongue nicker up and down her face and mouth, kiss kiss kiss; Phoenix, Luci, and Cherish look on with repulsed fascination.

Double ig, breathes Cherish.

There's some pretty wild shit a psychiatrist could dredge up about a bisexual lady who kisses snakes, says Luci.

Screw psychiatrists.

Pass.

Phoenix keeps sneaking looks at Luci, at the mouth which is sort of nondescript, the upper lip thin and narrow-cusped, the bottom lip a serviceable ledge. She is in a spasm of moral bewilderment, wondering if she's lesbian because she responded to Luci's kiss, or is the flesh that independent, can it react happily to anybody, anything? Looking at Luci, she decides she feels no desire, she'll hang out with Althea, have some more wine, pot, go back to her room.

Phoenix lies on the bed, watching the lit candles on the window sill. Althea's playing Velvet Underground, while Zuni oozes around in her lap, making Phoenix think of Deal's leather belt, how he'd jump it down her spine, drag it down her back before clapping her butt.

I think it's how they move.

What?

No arms or legs, no eyelids. Totally remote. They kill rodents and then just lie there. Snakes are unfairly linked to sin and seduction, the nasty stuff. Most cultures consider the serpent symbolic of rebirth, the circle eating its own tail. No one is indifferent to a snake.

What other jobs do you have, Althea?

102

One boring house-cleaning job and Mr. Yanakiam.

Who's he?

Oh god, he's one bizarre item, let me tell you.

Tell me.

Well, Mr. Gurgen Yanakiam hails from from Yugoslavia. He's 60, 65. His wife was a doctor but she died five years ago, and now he has me come over on Mondays. I clean for about an hour, nothing hard, since he barely exists—then comes the queer part. I go in his bedroom and put on one of his wife's outfits. He's got it all laid out on the bed, underwear, shoes, stockings, jewelry, dress, the works. Then I walk around the apartment while he pretends I'm her. No sex or anything. I keep my distance, my back to him. At five o'clock he goes out, I get undressed, take my fifty dollars off the dining room table, come back the next week. Plus I clean for this lady who's a Jungian analyst. She says she knew Jung in Switzerland. Incredibly dull, dull house, dull dust. I wonder if he was as dull as her?

Who, Carl Jung?

Yeah.

I couldn't say, I wasn't there.

Althea's gone up to Mt. Shasta for a week. Phoenix takes the city bus, following directions to Mr. Yanakiam's apartment. She's already cleaned the boring Jungian woman's apartment. Now she's headed to Gurgen's.

Althea coached her, do *not* let him hypnotize you, he'll try but you let him know right away you're tougher than him. I don't know what he'd do if you were in a trance or anything, so watch out, he's sneaky. Otherwise, it's a super-easy fifty dollars.

The apartment building is bismol pink, gaudy mica glitters in the stone. She pushes the buzzer beside G. Yanakiam. He opens the door with a gleeful face that collapses like cake the minute he sees her, or, rather, does not see Althea.

Who are you? a slabbed, guttural accent. Where's Althea?

Um, she had to go on vacation so she sent me. If you want, you can call me Althea.

No, no. This won't do. He is pouting; she straightens up, tries to seem tall as Althea, she worries he might sob.

Did she tell you what you do?

Everything.

Ok then, come in. I'm finishing my lunch. You can start with cleaning, then I see you in what, one hour's time?

Sure thing, Mr. Yanakiam.

Please. Gurgen. I'll be down there, he points down a dark sleeve of hall, in my office.

Ok, Gurgen.

Gurg (calling him that in her head) looks like a jack-o-lantern, orangeish brown skin, ballooning cheeks, tipped, fierce eyes.

Phoenix feels competent, cleaning. The risk of failure is so small, you can only improve things. Maybe she doesn't trust herself much beyond a shiny sink, a thought which startles her. She takes happy satisfaction, steering the vacuum in perfect overlapping stripes across his living room. Cleaning soothes like milk, unassailable activity. Maybe at its humblest, her character is most solid. In this apartment where nothing means anything to her,

104

the motions of cleaning tranquilize. Althea was right, the place is hardly lived in. A couple of dirty dishes, three or four crumbs on the linoleum, ashtrays to be dumped and rinsed, Gurg barely visits the planet.

At quarter to three, she opens the door to his bedroom. There is the outfit, like doll clothes, on the bed. A champagne-colored nubbly suit, boxy jacket with black saucer-buttons, rectangle skirt, lilac polyester blouse with pearl buttons and a floppy tie, gray pearl earrings, silk stockings and a grayed girdle, yellowed bra, lavender heels. Rowed neatly on the dressing table are a fuchsia lipstick, face powder in a mauvish shade called Rachel, purple eye shadow, eye pencil, an eyelash curler, and a bottle of TABU. Also on the dressing table is Gurg's wife, a photograph. Marcelled black hair, jaw set like a wrestler's, mean or pained eyes Phoenix can't tell, eyes she feels grimly spying as she unzips her jeans, tugs off her work shirt, kicks off her Dr. Scholl's. The bedroom, leaden blue drapes drawn, is 1940's, blonde sharp-cornered furniture, blue chenille bedspreads, little silk pillows like those square pastel candies her grandmother sets out in crystal dishes.

The clothes must be way too small for Althea. They sag on Phoenix, droop, air whistles between her and the suit. Rolling and pinning the waistband, folding the suit cuffs under. The make-up is the spookiest part, with Mrs. Y. looking on, humorless.

She klutzes out of the bedroom, high heels slippy, ankles wreaking, a doll tapping along the hall to the living room. Gurg, Mr. Yanakiam, does not keep his back to her as Althea had sworn he would. He does not ignore her. He is on the couch edge, eagerly observing, hands rhythmically working in his lap,

He half-stands, pats an ivory brocade chair across from him. She sits, x'es her legs at the ankles. Is she supposed to talk? Act like his wife? Damn, Althea. The clips on the earrings kill her earlobes.

So. You are Althea's friend? A hippie friend? I like the hippies. They are right to demand the freedoms, I agree with them. You

105

look very nice, very grown-up, in my wife's clothing. That is the suit she wore to medical conventions. My wife was a very formidable doctor, very intelligent in diagnosis. She studied in Yugoslavia as a young girl, pretty just like you, and then ... he stares intently at her face, she feels his lunch-breath as he talks about his wife, about Yugoslavia. She feels dozy, heavy—snap, idiot, the trance. Phoenix straightens up in the chair to see Gurgen's face one inch from hers, droning horribly. He is clad only in boxer shorts and dark blue socks.

She wrenches her arm out of his not very firm grasp and clips to the front door, grabbing her purse from the hall table.

Strong tea, he pleads from the center of his vacuumed carpet in filtered, lemon-scented light, pretending she has gone faint, is ill. The lardy toad in his underwear.

She ticks down the street in lavender heels, nylons swishing. God. After a while she slows, the shock receding. She yanks the earrings, whips them into already-littered shrubbery alongside a building, waits for a bus back to Shrader Street. Sits behind the driver in Mrs. Yanakiam's medical convention suit. She trips up the steps, runs into Althea's room, rips off the suit, girdle, nylons, hauling everything through the kitchen, plunging them viciously into a trashcan on the porch. Cherish and Luci are in the kitchen with friends, smoking and talking. Luci, studying her, says, far out make-up. You auditioning?

Too embarrassed to tell anybody. This feels as dumb as the time she gave meditation lessons in students' apartments and that Japanese guy, three feet tall and equally wide, spent the entire time chasing her through his apartment in too-tight underwear, until she had to climb out the bathroom window. Is she overly naive, too trusting, is that it? She didn't even get her super-easy fifty dollars.

Phoenix catches a short ride out of San Francisco along with some guy in burlap robes and a healing pendulum who informs her he's a seraphim. On a ramp outside Novato, they wait almost an hour before anybody stops. Phoenix, in a black mini-dress with beadwork all over the chest, Alpha boots, and a giant black hat of Althea's, picks up negative vibes about the one car that finally does squeal over, a cherry convertible with a pointy-faced driver. But her religious friend bunches up his burlap, plunks qualmless and seraphic in the front seat. Maybe her instincts are off, it's almost like she doesn't know anymore.

Where you two headed?

Fort Bragg.

Mendocino.

I'm headed to Cloverdale, that's inland a ways. I'll take you both up to Mendocino, howz that? Awhell, I can go on up to Bragg, no matter. He has a missing front tooth, and his eyes pinch at her right through dark glasses, making her recoil into the backseat.

Over the next three or so hours, Phoenix wistfully recalls caution and good sense. The second her door slams, he peels out like a speedboat, ninety miles an hour caroming in and out of lanes. Edging up to ask her robed companion something, hair painfully whipping her face, she sees a blue-black gun butt under the driver's mammoth thigh. He is gargantuan, with long mangly hair; the hair fooled her. He talks in his fast ratchety voice like he's trapped in a hamster wheel and loud enough so she hears the convertible's hot, and he's on parole for arson and deadly assault. Worse than what he says, he's obviously on some out-of-control death trip that would prefer company. Phoenix blasts north on Highway One, scared gelatinous.

Next he's drinking, getting whippier and loopier, veering the car close to cliffs, turning and rasty-grinning, "Anyone fixin' to die?"

Too late to get out of the car. Phoenix pictures them shooting off a cliff, somersaulting in the rubbery car, a red matchhead flipped into the sea. He giggles, steers straight awhile, skids the tires, grinning, "Who's for the big D?" Her hand is wet on the chrome handle, slippery with an insane faith she can bail out before the car goes over ... it's such a big car, there might be a few seconds.

In Mendocino, she crawls watery-kneed and nerve-dead from the car, which zips off in a cherry flash, the seraphim's face suspended above his robes, unperturbed. Shit, she left Althea's hat in the Cadillac, holding it between her feet the whole time because of the wind. Her knee caps vibrating, dizzy whorls at their centers, Phoenix closes herself in a phone booth, fishes up a quarter to call her sister.

Phoenix doesn't notice Carol's newest boyfriend drag up on a black motorcycle, leaving the motor whallop as he lopes over. She's hunkered over a free box outside the phone booth deciding between a Peruvian poncho and a red flannel cowboy shirt.

Mary Lou?

She jumps up, gripping the poncho.

Terry pumps her hand, polite as church and short as she is, with a rural freckly face, bandanna around his forehead.

My name's Phoenix.

Far out, but don't get all uptight if I forget. Carol always calls you Mary Lou.

Hooked to Terry's waist, her pelvis mashed against his butt, legs cocked back at the knees, she almost regrets the ride ending on a wavy gravy road in front of a tiny blue nick of a house.

Go on in. Carol's making your family's famous spaghetti and getting frantic, so it's good you're here.

Frantic about what—me?

Who else, vanishing and elusive sister?

I swear, my whole family thinks I'm helpless.

I'm doubt that.

Damn straight.

Carol swings out the screen door just as Phoenix climbs the porch, so they wind up colliding more than embracing. Their timing's always been off. Different brain waves, thinks Phoenix. Carol's welcome has a sisterly chomp.

Wow, Mary Lou, have you been sleeping by the road, in the road, or what? She runs her hand down Phoenix's hair, crinkles up her face. Maybe a bath before dinner? Hey Ter, think there's enough hot water for Mary Lou?

Terry's on the sidelines of a huge vegetable garden, spading compost.

Could be. He looks up, grins. Better ask her other name.

Carol tugs her into the house. I'll show you how the hot water works … backwards. What's your other name?

Never mind.

Come on. Tell me.

I just kinda picked it.

So?

Don't laugh.

I promise. Come *on,* Mary Lou.

Phoenix.

Oh. Carol sighs, stops fussing with the shower, looks back over her shoulder. Long auburn hair, delicate lavenderish face, an impossible person to be around without feeling smaller and smaller on the inside, big and cloddish outside.

Mom and Dad have been so freaked. I keep telling them to relax, you'll grow out of it. So make me right. You turn the cold for hot but just halfway. Here's a tiny heater for extra warmth. Oh, and a towel.

How long have you lived here?

I left the houseboat in Sausalito six months ago. Terry's been with me the whole time, remember I told you how we met the night he got back from India? Hey, before you came in, did you notice how shrunken the pine trees are? Because of weird minerals in the soil, all the trees are stunted. Even our vegetables are pygmies. It's a trip. Well, I'll leave you to clean up. Have you got other clothes?

Yeah.

Where?

My pack.

Oh. Far out. Well, enjoy your bath and we're glad you made it here ok. Later we'll get stoned, discuss our love lives.

Mm.

Carol's bumped her right back in place—little sister, the one to cluck over, reduce by worrying about. When she strips off her jeans, Phoenix sees the wet maroon stain. Thankyou god, put a comic strip balloon over her head with *Whew!* inside it. She hunts around the little bathroom, finds a Tampax box behind the toilet. Carol's got everything lined up, organized as math, efficient. A glass vase with wildflowers in the window. Artistic, too. No physical evidence of Terry. Either he's neater than Carol or she won't let him in here.

"If not for you, babe I couldn't find the door
couldn't even see the floor
I'd be sad and blue
If not for you—"

Terry and her sister are bopping goofily to Dylan when Phoenix comes out of the bathroom. All three of them go at it, the floor quaking, until Terry hauls Carol down in the big rocker for a smooch … oooh whee ride me high, tomorrow's the day my bride's gonna come, oooh no, we're gonna fly, down in the easy chair … the spaghetti smell lays a head trip on Phoenix. Mom's Sunday night spaghetti. Her job, the garlic butter.

That's some get-up. Carol looks fish-faced, sloppy-speeched. Stoned.

Like it? I turned the poncho upside down for a skirt.

Most brilliant. Carol glances up at Terry's chin. My sister's famous for her fashion flair.

It's cute. An upside down poncho.

It itches like crazy right through my tights. Want me to make garlic bread?

I did already. Mom always had you do that, right?

Yeah. God Carol, your house. It's so neat. So perfect. Like a magazine or something. She had intended to compliment her sister, but it came out tweaked, with an edge that Carol would not miss.

Carol's expensive brass bed has a blue-and-white quilt, the floors are varnished pine, two blue-striped armchairs sit by the fireplace. Wild flowers everywhere. Carol used to do window displays for a ritzy store in San Francisco. Now she sells handmade baby quilts in local galleries, can't keep up with her orders.

Terry tries helping Phoenix out, as if he sees how deflating it can be, being Carol's sister. She appreciates his empathy, actually, she likes him.

So tell us, how's life on the highway?

God, Mom's so paranoid, she keeps sending the Red Cross out after you.

What's it like, Phoenix? Terry remembers to call her that. Carol sticks to Mary Lou.

Well, I haven't been raped, murdered, or given bad acid, so there's not much point to Mom and Dad's hassling you.

Carol sits on Terry's lap, vaguely sulky, while Terry asks questions.

Do you hitch rides until you feel like stopping somewhere? Where do you stay? What about money?

Phoenix explains how going the way the Universe is going, floating in its current, you can't get hurt. Money will appear, enough to get you by, and people give you stuff when you need it.

Your little sister is living according to classic Eastern philosophy, submissive to Fate, to the divine plan, all very Hindu. Most Westerners can't deal with passivity. We hurl ourselves into the world, attack the temporal instead of allowing it to unfold. You've probably lived past lives in India.

Maybe. Hey Carol, remember how I used to go around talking with an English accent, and getting travel books out of the library on England, saying I was homesick? Weird. I bet it's true, reincarnation.

No, but I do remember when you made us say grace every night, the same time you'd decided to be a nun, and we all had to bow our heads and mumble along. Mom was barely tolerant, blaming Daddy for keeping you in that Catholic school. Oh, wow, speaking of fate …

What?

I just thought of somebody you *have* to meet. Ter, wouldn't Flash be perfect for Mary Lou? Are we not talking destiny and karma?

Terry belches, winks at Phoenix, who winks right back.

Next afternoon destiny and karma locate Flash, through her sister. They've stopped in a hotel bar in town when suddenly Carol jumps a guy in a red fireman's shirt and cowboy hat, whumping him on the shoulder.

Far out, babe, we were just heading out to your place. I want my crazy little sister to meet you.

Flash turns to see her crazy little sister. A fairly wincing introduction, so Phoenix bends down, nudging a nonexistent rock from her shoe.

They tail Flash's mud-brown truck, his two dogs in the back waltzing, skittering on sharp turns, heading into thick, cathedral-high redwoods.

Flash lives here for now, it's a place that gets passed along.

A homemade lighthouse, Phoenix thinks, a wooden obelisk. Flash's truck is angled in front. She follows Carol into the gnome-ish first level with its dirt floor, woodstove, single chair and funky table. Rough-cut stairs spiral to a loft, a square room with floor-to-ceiling glass on two sides. Outside are shaggy redwoods and a weak, rinsed-looking sky. There's a bed, a rocking chair, a woodstove, a Confederate flag above the bed. Phoenix is tripping on the view when she sees Carol, foreshortened, the top of her sister's head holding a coin of sun, walking to her van, getting in and putzing off.

Slowed by the seashell whorl of stairs, she's outside in time to see the yellow rump of Carol's van switching between trees, gone down a trail of thickly needled red clay. Flash, his timing canny, veers around the corner, split kindling heaped against his red chest, his shoulder-length hair amber-flecked, his expression predatory.

He grins. Guess she thought we'd get better acquainted by ourselves.

Carol abandoned her. She can't believe this. Phoenix doesn't resist his sex, so like his face, fierce, brief, numbing. Afterward, he's complacent, discussing himself at length while the woodstove gives out patches of heat, the windows obsidian, eye-like.

Phoenix, still in the earliest, most aching hours of her period, is amazed he doesn't care. He was a medic in Nam, what blood she puts on him or his bed he says is nothing.

In the morning, she's disoriented, her mouth parched and sour, teeth furred. The woodstove is out, air against her face feels raw and blue. She hears him downstairs, cowboy-singing, then ratcheting up the stairs, kissing her ferociously.

Owwwow. God, your whiskers are like toothpicks. What are those?

These? He traces a saddle of blue spots across his nose. Gunpowder. I was a mighty dangerous kid, into homemade explosives. When I was nine, I invented this little toy cannon for the Fourth of July. I was out in the driveway, kneeling like an idiot in front of the muzzle, lighting it, when ka-boom … blew up my face. My mother, driving in from the store, sees me screaming, face all peckered with blood and powder, and we spend half the night in the emergency room, doctors picking powder out of my face, using tweezers. What you see is what they couldn't dig down to.

Blue freckles.

Yeah. Blue freckles.

Cute.

Argh, not cute. C'mon downstairs, here, put this on you. He hands her a gigantic flannel bathrobe. Breakfast is served.

Flash hums operatically, conducting a grungy spatula over his fried potatoes, fried eggs, boiling coffee. Shows her how he slits the jellied whites with a knife so they cook faster. They carry plates outside, sit back to back on a huge crumbly stump, shoveling food, the air spicy with redwood, sunlight buckling them at the shoulders. The eggs have black specks, the potatoes are half raw, Phoenix unloads everything into her mouth with rapt greed.

Later, when he drives away to see friends up north and cut firewood, she climbs the tower, the silence hard, an aggressive punch in her ears. She looks at his things and touches, they have a simplicity that moves her. She likes things that belong to other people, that have no memory, no reverberation. Lies down a minute

114

on the bed, feeling air shrink around her. After awhile, spirals back downstairs, slaps freezing water to her face, drags at her hands with a sliver of gray gritty soap. The water makes her gasp, pinks up her hands. Heading into the woods in a pair of Flash's jeans and fireman's shirt with a roll of toilet paper, she feels clean, how an animal might feel, stilled to immediate hearing, seeing. Wishes she lived here, that Flash might not ever return, wanting stuff from her.

He comes back after dark, with his dogs and a truckload of wood; she feigns sleep up in the freezing tower. She listens to him tromp up, light the woodstove. He comes across the room, sits on her.

Whoah, didn't know anybody was home. Hey, brought you a present. Holds out a box of Tampax.

You hungry? I've got bread and cheese and tomato soup downstairs.

They eat cheese and bread on the crumpled bloodied bed, feeding one another, turning silly. Flash hooks her panties off the floor with his big toe, tugs them over his head so the crotch runs like a road stripe along the top of his head ... fake-falls from the bed, dances naked in her boots, spills her purse, seizes the makeup. He has her put lipstick on his mouth, kohl on his eyes, fluffs his hair. He bellows apelike, lunking on and off the bed, pounding his chest. In raggedy gold-and-black stove light, they tip backward on the bed, locked like bugs, licking makeup and sweat. His back feels filmy, gritty, steamy, heat slips off her fingers from his back. His body is bunched with noise and movement, gruntings, rubbings, suspended archings, eyes catlike, kohl-striped, indifferent. She watches him, fascinated, feels second-hand excitement from what is happening, nothing more. They share a joint, her thighs gleaming and sticky, in firelight.

Flash talks around the smoke in his mouth.

It all happens together. like there's no time. Everything runs together, but we, as fearful humans, divide it like real estate, with logic.

He exhales.

Alan Watts, do you know who he is, he thinks we put this uh, *grid* of logic over what are basically waves ... we crank life through this grid that doesn't exist except in our heads. The idea of life being waves unsettles people, the idea that maybe there's no order or logic out there.

He tokes again, mumbles, grabs and kisses her hand with his red-stained mouth.

Come on. Wrap yourself in my blanket, we'll go out, find us some good stars.

First thing I noticed was how guys with blond hair, especially the ones taller than me, got picked off first. First time in my life I felt ok about being short. Yellow hair was this perfect target.

Both dogs were snuffing and trampling in the darkness, then flopping loose beside him, eyes shiny, breath meaty, devoted.

How long were you there?

Two years three months.

Did you work out of a hospital?

Nope. I scooped hits, triage, which means you decide who dies in what order. Judge and jury in the field.

Sounds horrible.

Does it? Try insane. Three, four guys get hit, you have to know in a split second who to treat first, providing you can even get to them through the automatic fire.

Did you know the people you treated?

Mostly yes, which made for a lot of morally gray decisions. Two guys I got to know pretty well, one like me, from Louisiana, a Baton Rouge Cajun, and this other dude from Pensacola, Florida, we used to call it Pepsicola, both took the same land mine. The Cajun guy had both legs blown off at the hips, he split into three equally ugly pieces. The other dude was possibly gonna make it, he had a fair chance. I knew that. My brain knew that. But I couldn't leave the Cajun guy, it was like it was me or my family or something? It was weird. I kept slapping him with tourniquets, morphine packets, everything in my pack I'm sticking in him or on him. I even turned his legs, to see which way they'd fit back on, while right behind me the second guy's crying, yelling for help. That was the worst. I don't know what happened to me.

Did he die?

Who? My friend? Shit, he was dead before I got there. The Florida guy died an hour later, because I didn't treat him.

God, Flash.

Yeah. I screwed up. I don't sleep, thinking about it, trying to figure out why I worked on a dead man and left the other guy to die. I mean I basically killed him.

118

Phoenix strokes one of the dogs, her thumb denting into a bump above one eye socket, her hand pushing hard across the dog's knobbed, sweaty skull.

Their lives were wasted. No different than if they'd been blown to bits in a robbery or on the freeway by some drunk. No different at all.

Did you ever get hurt? Wounded?

Never, which made me paranoid. When you first get there, you feel marked, like there's this big red bull's-eye around you saying shoot me. When you get over that, you start to feel a little reckless, then you can die that way. I must have been invisible the entire time. Bronchitis, that was it, all I ever had, a mild case. What teachers, parents, boy scouts, coaches, and dancing school taught you don't count for a flying fuck over there. You react to whatever's happening at that moment, you do whatever it takes to keep breathing. I could feel good and heroic one minute, then turn and do some stupid stunt out of a terror I couldn't have believed. They say war's the ultimate extreme, and that's goddamn true. There's supposed to be some great military discipline, this efficient regimentation, but the fact is most soldiers are secret anarchists and war will twist you into any damn thing it wants.

Flash pushes his hand over her heart. In my opinion, we're all evil as Hitler and if we're never tested, we can get pretty righteous. I saw guys killed saving a buddy about as much as I saw guys, sometimes the very same ones, dive behind a buddy in order to live one more day. It would be one way one minute, then reverse. We all got morally grayed, capable of anything. Just before I left, I found this little kid in the road. His village had been torched. He orbited around me, a little shadow, ate with me, slept by me. I guess we'd killed his mother, his father, his brothers and sisters, grandmother, grandfather, cousins, aunts, uncles, destroyed his home, food, clothes, everything—and this little guy, he was about five or six, just clung to me. He and I got into this way of sleeping with our arms and legs around each other, kind of how me and my little brother used to sleep.

Flash's voice drops off. His back is to her.

What happened? To the little boy?

He shrugs.

She inches forward. I'm sorry, you don't have to tell me. Want to go back? It's getting cold.

Goddamn fucking-ass war. Flash is up, pounding his fist against a tree, incoherent.

The dogs, heads cocked, thunk tails in cold dirt.

Phoenix gets up, wraps the blanket around her and Flash, shutting out the world.

Journeybook

Rimbaud says the Visionary becomes Monstrous in order to glimpse the Sublime. This earth-world, flesh-consciousness, is beauty and pain, beauty and pain, beauty and pain, ebony and bone spokes in a blurring wheel, circling toward what loss? I have been three days and nights in a wooden tower, looking out at a black spiky sea of woods to a blue heel of water, a desert of traitorous skies … is there no truth, no order, no Design, or is it above our human capacity to visualize or to understand? Each of us a molecule, a cell, an atom blindly limited within the limitless God….When I have seen enough, done enough, had enough— "O Sounds and Visions!"—I will sit somewhere, anywhere, and *write*. When the horrible issue of myself has gone, when I am done with vanishing, I will *speak*. I have emptied myself, being magnified for some greater Purpose. The visionary blind, the poet mute, the oceans of silence before poetry.

I am not happy. (Is that the point? The family album, the school photograph, smile, smile or it will disappoint!)

I am accused of thinking too much, feeling too much.

No mirrors hang in this tower. One is reflected everywhere, nowhere.

The dress has a dozen gauzy layers of black from the waist to the ankles, sleeves like vermilion wings, their cuffs embellished and heavy with gold stitching. Brass bells, small as birdshot, are sewn around the deep, gold-embroidered hem.

God, this weighs tons. It's gorgeous. A wedding dress from where?

Afghanistan. It's from the 1920's.

She shakes the hem. It sounds like Christmas, I love it. How could you have enough money for this?

Questions like that are as stupid as calling me cute.

Lifting her in his arms like a curl of melon, Flash dumps her on the bed, pulling the big flannel shirt up over her head, knotting the sleeves so her head's muffled in red flannel. Sunlight makes a polleny square across her breasts.

Mmm, nummy num num, he talks to the breasts, nipping and growling, tickling until she screeches and bucks, accidentally kneeing him.

Argh, what a treacherous thing you show yourself to be, my darling love.

Help. Let me out, her voice is muzzled in flannel. Flash, let me out, it isn't funny, she giggles, I can't breathe.

At twilight, the brown truck jolts out of the woods, idling on the troughed road so they can suck up the end of a joint prior to heading into town. Right on top of the familiar-to-monotonous ocean, clouds sit in fuchsia tufts, poodle heads, she giggles, they look like poodle heads with those dinky pom poms. Flash poodlebarks, leans over, nipping at her shoulder.

They park in front of a famous tourist hotel with ornate Victorian railings. Flash is taking her to dinner.

The dining room is empty, abusively air-conditioned. Phoenix notices a long white table marked reserved, set for six. Flash tows her by the finger to a corner table in the back. The waitress slouches over, giving Flash a peck on the top of his head.

Hi, darlin. He squeezes her knotty waist. This is Phoenix.

122

Far out dress. The waitress is so hostile, Phoenix figures she has probably slept with Flash. This town is one humongous bed, Carol told her, laughing. Anybody here over six weeks is guaranteed a case of gonorrhea.

We'll have wine to start, that suit you, babe?

But Phoenix doesn't care about wine, her attention is over Flash's left shoulder, fixed on her sister and Terry standing with two other people. Carol turns to say something to these people. Phoenix recognizes her mother and father, dressed up, peering anxiously around.

What? Flash follows her gaze.

It's my *parents*. Holy shit. Phoenix knocks her chair back, fumbles for her purse, all the bells on her hem ringing with alarm. Flash's hand catches her.

Hey, where you goin? smoothly giving himself away.

You knew?

Shh. They just want to see for themselves that you're all right. So. Why don't you look all right?

You don't understand. You don't understand what this means, dammit.

But she is held there by Flash, made to wait.

Sorry, sweet, he whispers. Now smile because here they come.

Her mother's face is bunched, clogged with emotions, her father's absorbed, talking to Terry. He scarcely glances at her.

Look Mother, says Carol. Tah-dah. Here she is. Perfectly healthy.

Oh honey. Mary Lou. Oh honey. We've been terribly worried. Her mother catches her in a brittle hug, her affection like Carol's, conditioned by disapproval. She tilts back to study her daughter's face, tracing a baby fingertip under one eye, rimmed with black kohl.

Terry bounces forward, grinding his palms together, acting diplomatic. Ah, everybody, table's already reserved. Joining us, Flash?

This was set up. Arranged. Flash knew. Everyone knew. They had tricked her.

She and Flash sit together, her mother and Carol across, her father to the right and on the left, Terry, maintaining a tactful performance.

This is a four-star restaurant, Mrs. Temple. The grilled salmon is outstanding.

With a lopsided facial twitch meant to convey she is not so easily won, Mrs. Temple receives the menu from the waitress who's bumping her hip into Flash while being eyed by Mr. Temple with the sort of moist leer Phoenix remembers painfully.

Flash hoists a wine bottle in one hand, a glass in the other, smirking nervously.

Anyone for vino?

No thank you, young man, her father glances with masterful irony over his bifocals. Not just yet. No sand dabs on the menu?

No, not tonight, sir. But our paella is delicious, very fresh. And I'll get you the wine list.

The menu is an object for Phoenix to hang onto. Her chest feels pumped, her fingers prickly from overbreathing. Carol is on some fake social trip; Phoenix half-expects her to hiss across the table, give me a break, Mary Lou, and act a little less bizarre so they'll stop hassling me.

Phoenix. The name lumps up in her mouth, a failed charm. Not wayward, irresponsible, impractical, neurotic, not what they think or say. *They do not know ME.* She sees her parents with the acuity of rage, counts strand upon strand of her father's rumpled, graying hair, can count and separate, a feat pleasing to a professor of higher mathematics, a man curt with those unable to lock into clean lines, finite sums. A man impeccable in his lust for women. He understands and approves of Carol, his sensible, beautiful daughter, but this other scraggly sheep, who is this disheveled, intense creature lacking logic's fine grace? Her world is a chaos, formless as seawater, it cannot match his, an elegant cold grid.

Oh piffle, her mother's knee-jerk reaction to untoward emotion. Piffle-twaffle, let's not get carried away. She taught kindergarten. An orthopedic shoe contained her left foot. Phoenix used to shut herself in her parents' closet to spy on the shoe, black drab beetle. Other mothers with syrup-colored calves wearing heels or strappy sandals, pretty jots of toe polish; her mother dragging the shoebeast, the foot botched and clumsy. In an intelligent, uncompromising way, her mother could be considered attractive, silver-brown hair fat in a ponytail, her one cosmetic a blue-red lipstick. She is wearing a burgundy wool dress, an amber bead necklace Phoenix remembers from her dresser. Phoenix and Carol had been reared in a state of drained fluorescence, in school hallways and vacant classrooms, at night, with other children whose parents scheduled and attended political meetings and rallies and marches. These children tended to be precocious, undisciplined, runny-nosed, overtired. She, Carol, the others, hauled along in wagons with crepe, waving banners and slogans, needing to pee; meals missed, dishes slopped all over, the meetings came first. Social justice outweighed any domestic routine. More recently, her mother went alone, her father closing himself further into numbers, working late, light piking like bronze under his study door. Her mother volunteers at a draft counseling center, Phoenix imagines her efficient compassion. All Carol's friends, then all of hers, confided in Mrs. Temple what they could never tell their own mothers, accepting her counsel on birth control, suicide, abortion, drugs, failure in school. Mary Lou, a product of politically liberal, activist parents, wasn't supposed to have problems, to reflect poorly. She understood. She'd never told her mother a thing.

The expensive wine arrives.

John, a toast? Mrs. Temple lofts her glass. The others follow, except Phoenix. Noting this, her father smiles grimly.

Here's to finding our youngest in one piece, here's to being together, here's to an end to the goddamned war, and here's to what looks like damned good paella.

Everyone except Phoenix laughs. Mrs. Temple leans across the table.

Mary Lou, darling. Don't put such a face on. It's pre-adolescent, angel. We just needed to see you with our own eyes. Carol's vague reassurances weren't enough.

I'm fine.

I'm sure you think so, but really sweetie, you don't look healthy to me. Dark circles under your eyes and your skin's pasty. I wonder what you're eating.

Phoenix shrugs, looks up, smiles. I'm eating paella.

Honey, we drove up to see you and Carol for another reason. Your grandmother's had quite a bad stroke and we'd like you and Carol to drive down with us to the hospital to see her. It may be for the last time.

Numbness fills her fingers, she's lost control of her breathing, gulping, then forgetting. Her mother hates her grandmother.

And sweetie. We want you to come home for a bit. You don't have to go back to school right away. We'll help you find a job. Maybe it's the pressure, children are under terrible pressure these days. Wouldn't you like to come home with us, until things clear up a bit for you?

Bringing me home won't change anything.

They both punch at their salads, silent.

Mom. I'm fine. I know how to take care of myself. I'm meeting a lot of people …

This is what your father and I are afraid of.

I haven't had one bad experience.

Oh honey, you're awfully naive, that's why we worry so. A young girl traveling alone, and Carol says you sometimes hitchhike—

You can tell who's safe.

Pete's sake, Mary Lou, that's like saying you know how not to get pregnant without using birth control.

Anne, let's keep it down, shall we? We promised ourselves a pleasant dinner, wasn't that right? Have you told her yet about the job I've lined up for her in the Physics Lab? She can come back with us tonight, start work next week, they'd love to have

126

her. Your mother and I agree perhaps more therapy, we're happy to pay for help for you, Mary Lou. Get you back on track.

We love you darling, her mother says softly.

Downing air, the fingers of one hand numbing on the fork, the other hand clawed in her lap. My grandmother. Grandmother. Oh.

Carol goes for a rescue.

Mom, Dad. Don't push her. Be happy she's here, safe, having dinner with us. We can discuss things back at my house if you'd like. Anyway, it might help if you call her by her new name.

Her parents look startled.

What? her mother says. What?

Mary Lou? What's Carol saying? Do you have some other name? You aren't married I hope.

Flash turns informer. She likes being called Phoenix.

My Lord, her mother says. I've had enough of this identity changing.

Anne, I'm hopeful Mary Lou will be capable of explaining what this means, naming herself after a mythical bird.

The waitress shows up grinning, completely incongruous.

How's dinner, everyone?

Mr. Temple, pink napkin tucked rakishly in his shirt, tips back in his chair and eyes the waitress's breasts.

Heavenly.

Carol rolls her eyes, laughs. Really. Dad is just the dirtiest old man.

Yes, isn't he, Mrs. Temple says with trained humor.

I don't think it's funny.

Piffle, Mary Lou. Don't take everything so seriously.

I'm sorry, I do take everything seriously. Life is serious.

She has a point, Terry comments drily, gently.

Flash chews noisily, crashing seafood into his mouth.

Carol sighs, pops holes in the tablecloth with her fork.

Mr. Temple's fork is suspended between the table and his mouth. What's the matter with her? Has she been smoking that

127

stuff, that pot? He looks coldly at Phoenix, then at his wife, expecting her to quell this ridiculous outburst. He moves the fork to his mouth.

Mary Lou. Please. You're just terribly young and you don't understand. We've been worried to death about you these past months, never hearing a word, not one phone call, the burden all on Carol, it was quite selfish behavior, Mary Lou. Quite immature. I suggest you look at your own behavior before judging the rest of us. And this business of changing your name. I don't know. I don't understand it at all....I am glad to see you in a dress, though. It's been years.

Carol is looking with concern at Phoenix.

Want me to go with you into the bathroom a minute?

She shakes her head.

Flash nudges her, mouth crammed. Hey, lighten up. Just the folks.

She ignores him. He lied. He brought her here. Her grandmother is dying.

This group needs more wine. Where is our waitress? You notice, Terry, boy is she stacked. What a pair on her.

This is her father, tongue out, chewing paella. Her mother, whispering, distraught, with Carol. Flash grabbing the waitress by the butt as she passes. Terry quiet.

God, I hate you, I hate all of you. She scrapes her chair back. Just leave me the fuck alone....hears her mother, John, go and get her. Well, he won't, she knows that. He has never once gone and got her. He loathes these scenes, her.

She crosses the wood porch, runs down steps to the beach. She has no feeling in her hands, her feet trip on kelp-littered sand, the water, its heavy slap and dark noise big as her anger. Anger, grief, and fiery solitude. There is integrity in being misunderstood, a swath of fierce silence conceals you.

She half listens for footsteps. There's no sound, no one coming. Well, fuck them. That's all. Fuck them.

Journeybook

You are in someone's old wedding dress, a bride dead or perhaps dying ... You open calm arms, your spine is made of the moon, you practice your child's ballet, a ballerina under streetlights. You see them, the figures of your family, mother, father, sister, like gathered dark blossoms on the white porch, watching, knowing they have caught you, heart sticking to the sweet, sad lure of your grandmother. They are shadows who held you briefly. You embrace them with your arms—*port de bras*—you lift them to the stars, one leg upraised for flight—arabesque—you bow to the ocean, cross the little highway toward those who claim you again and again, even as they lose you, have lost you.

Journeybook

We are in a hospital room with one white bed. She is strapped into a plain dark chair.

I kneel before her in love.